“Reflections Of A Hummingbird”

M L Curtis

M.L.C. (Hom) Dip Hyp ISCH

Acclaimed Author of

“The Goldfish That Jumped,”

“The Kingfisher That Rocked”

& “From Stuck Duck To Hummingbird.”

First published in the United Kingdom by
ML Curtis October 2017

First edition

ISBN 978-0-9933734-6-6

Published by ML Curtis

"The Reflections Of A Hummingbird"

"Our deepest fear is not that we are inadequate. Our deepest fear is that we are powerful beyond measure. It is our light - not our darkness that most frightens us. Your playing small does not serve the world, there's nothing enlightened about shrinking so that people won't feel insecure around you. We were all meant to shine as children. It's not just in some of us, it's in everyone, and, as we let our own light shine we unconsciously give others permission to do the same. As we are liberated from our own fear, our presence automatically liberates others."

Marianne Williamson.

This book is dedicated to Diane Mather and my dearest grandmother. Thank you for leaving me with precious memories, your profound love and deep wisdom.

CONTENTS

Part 1

Chapter One

"Papa was a rolling stone. Wherever he lay his hat was his home, and when he died, all he left us was alone" rang out from the stereo, as Elizabeth lay on the bed in tears once again. Another row and another broken heart, she felt she was being punished for something of which she was totally unaware. She lay there, not for the first time this week, month or year, trying to gain control of a multitude of emotions, as they threatened to engulf her whole being.

Yet another relationship breakdown, what was it that had gone so wrong this time? Was it her? She was the common denominator after all. Five failed relationships in as many years. Why was it that everyone else seemed to have the perfect relationship, perfect children and the perfect life?

What was it that was holding her back from finding her dream partner? Robert had seemed so perfect when they had first met. Looking at him across the room whilst at her friend's apartment at the house-warming seemed to breathe a spark of life into her, after she had spent the last eighteen months single.

Elizabeth was a thirty something and felt very much as though she was a no-body. She had been married to Ted for just over five years, when they had just seemed to drift apart. He had worked away and stayed away even when he was home. She fell in love with him the first time they had met at a mutual friends' birthday party over twelve years ago.

All this woman had ever wanted was to be loved and to love. Was that really too much to ask from life, the world, the universe?

Why was life so complicated? Why were people cruel and heartless at times? What was going on that had caused her so much pain? she felt that she had always played by society's rules and had towed the line. She had been a good wife, cook, domestic Goddess and she felt a good mother when her two boys had arrived into the world. She felt her parents were great role models and both had attended church every Sunday without fail. They were well-respected in the community and had a good marriage.

Why? Oh why was this happening to her? What had she done to deserve this? What had she done to deserve any of this?

She quickly moved in to the en-suite, as she wretched into the toilet bowl. Although the toilet was clean, even the smell of it caused even more nausea. Bile was the only thing to come up, though she felt like her whole intestines could at any given moment become part of the toilet bowl. Clinging to the bowl, she realised that not only was her heart ripped to shreds, but now she also felt that her whole-body systems were broken.

Eventually the intensity of the feelings eased slightly as she lay perspiring on the bed. Her sons were with their paternal grandmother, whom she had always disliked and yet liked in another way. Weird that she would think of her at this time? She was due to collect them the following afternoon. She looked across at her bedside cabinet and saw a photo of her pride and joy. The twins were born only minutes apart and were her sanity – at least they were most of the time. Now aged eight, and soon to be nine, she had a birthday party to plan and presents to buy.

Suddenly the distraction of thinking of her boys sent a huge emotional wave right through her body and she was once again engulfed in emotion. She physically quivered and her body shook as if to acknowledge the extremities of what she was experiencing. As doubt, guilt, fear, worry and the unknown, not to mention a whole heap of emotions that she didn't even understand, nor could she label as such, rippled through her being, she caught a glimpse of a star through the open window. It was a beautiful clear night and the open windows allowed in a welcome breeze on this Summers' evening. August was a special month for her as her boys would turn nine in just over a month.

The sight of the evening star brought a very welcome momentary distraction from her intense emotional state. As she looked up, it felt powerful and seemed to bring an air of peacefulness into the whole room. She instantly dismissed the feelings, just as she dismissed all her feelings and, just as she was about to turn away, she saw it move. Was it a falling star? Did they actually exist? She had always been told to ignore suspicious nonsense and believed that they didn't exist. Could it be? It seemed to move at rocket speed through the darkness of the evening. Being the great sceptic that she was, she felt she didn't believe in any of that *weird stuff* and yet, if it could be true, that she was allowed just *one wish upon that falling star?*

Dare she really make a wish? It was moving so fast that it would soon be out of sight. "Wake me up from this nightmare that I'm living," were the words uttered from her mouth, before she had even realized what she had said. She had always felt that she was in control of her life and the things she said and did, and yet, without hesitation she had uttered those words of absolute desperation. No sooner had they left her lips, than her eyes closed and she drifted into one of the deepest sleeps she had ever experienced.

Chapter Two

The following day she awoke to find herself in exactly the same position in which she had drifted off to sleep. She was feeling different yet wasn't sure why and not being one to be taken up by her emotions, she dismissed these feeling, brushing them off as she always did. Yet, she felt peaceful and calm which certainly wasn't Elizabeth. Always in control and always ready to prove herself to anyone, she had controlled every single aspect of her life so far. Well, at least she had certainly tried.

Yet, she had to agree that feeling calm and peaceful, after the previous night's events was quite a welcome feeling. She wondered how to control this and confusion began to creep into her thoughts. How could she feel calm? Why would she feel calm? She had just broken up with someone she had loved. He had quite clearly stated that he wanted absolutely nothing more to do with her.

She should feel emotionally battered and feel wretched. Yet, she did not. Instead she felt calm and peaceful. She always had a plan for the day and her previous plan had been that her and her lover would make love through the evening, then again in the morning, before she had to organize collecting her sons.

So, now she had no plans, apart from collecting the boys at 4pm. It was a little over approximately thirty minute drive to her ex-mother-in-law's place and she glanced over at the clock to see that it was 10am. She was always up before 7am. What was happening to her? She wandered into the en-suite and looked at the mascara, which was streaked down her face. By now usually she had had a morning run and done her stretches, not to mention put on a load in the washing machine and made the house look perfect.

As she looked in the mirror wondering whether to go for a bath or a run, she actually felt she heard someone say *"reflect."* She was looking into the mirror after all...at her less than perfect reflection. Well, it would be once she put on her make-up and did her hair. She distinctly heard the word uttered again *"reflect."* 'Umm' she thought to herself, probably just the breeze through the still open windows. She moved into the other room to close them. Yet they were already closed and she recalled looking through them at the falling star the previous evening. She had then drifted off and slept well over her usual time. She certainly had not closed the windows.

Returning to look in the mirror she saw herself as the imperfect creature she was, at least without make-up. Soon, with her magic concealer, foundation, blusher, eye shadow and eye-liner, a little mascara, lip liner and lip gloss, she'd both look and feel wonderful. She heard the birds outside tweeting much more loudly than usual as if the local cat was on the prowl. She became so distracted by their noise that she forget to put on her make-up, as she would normally have done by now.

She decided to go for a run. Needless to say, this particular morning after being so distracted, she left without even wearing her lippy.

'Another day and another broken relationship' she thought. She then realised that she hadn't checked her mobile phone. In fact, where was it? In her handbag? The pocket of her tight, skinny jeans? On the dressing table?

Another weird moment she thought, as she realised that normally she had it right on the bedside cabinet. She was usually looking over it the moment she awoke in order to catch up on Facebook and Twitter for gossip and news updates. She often had a message waiting for her from Robert. The phone was in the lounge, which was certainly odd, as she didn't recall leaving it on the coffee table. Looking through it, she sighed as she acknowledged with great sadness that the inbox was clearly *empty.*

They had argued last night at the party and she was so embarrassed when he raised his voice in front of her friends. Surely, they would have wanted to know how she was this morning? Surely? She decided that there must be something wrong with the phone, so she switched it off, then plugged it into the charger and waited for the usual pings, notifying her of incoming messages. Nothing. Not a whisper. She repeated the process. Switching it off and on twice. Still nothing. She decided to go for her run, leaving it on the table and then maybe she would call the network later, to ensure it was working properly.

Trees lined the road that led into the local park. Setting out for her run she felt the warm breeze against her skin. This was a new experience for her, as usually she was wrapped up in thoughts of the day. Which friends she would meet and impress. Who would be choosing the local cafes, bars or restaurants for their lunch and who would have the gossip from the party last night. 'Shit' she thought, 'I'm the local gossip.'

Her eyes were beginning to water from the bright sunshine, as she ran closer towards the park. She could hear children laughing and birds tweeting, people talking and dogs barking, in a fun kind of way. "What the hell" she actually said out loud as she realised that she had left her mobile phone back at the house. Thus, for the first time in years she was running without earplugs listening to Beyonce, Emile Sande or the local most popular radio station.

She repeated "What the hell" again and was surprised to hear her own voice. Usually the ear plugs drowned out everything. Elizabeth liked to live life to the full and loved playing music loudly. There were now so many new experiences for her, as she became more aware of her surroundings. She had never seen the birds in the park, yet alone acknowledged them. She was startled and jumped as she heard some nearby ducks quacking loudly, whilst trying to reach the nuts and seeds a little boy was throwing for their breakfast.

In that startled moment she lost her footing and tripped over some loose stones. She landed in an awkward position and sat completely unladylike at the side of the path. She took in a deep breath and sat there watching, as the little child continued to feed the ducks. She didn't realise that her ankle was beginning to swell and it was only as the child was ushered away by his father, that she remembered where she was. As she placed her hands by her side to lift herself to her feet, she noticed an outstretched hand reaching down towards her. Without thinking, she took the hand and looked up into the eyes of a middle aged Mediterranean man. As he helped her to her feet, he explained that he had watched her slip a few minutes ago. He had become concerned when she had not got back up again. He was at that time on the other side of the pond, so had it had taken him a little while to walk around to reach her.

"Thank You" she said as she tried to put weight on her foot. It gave way and she shrieked when a searing pain ripped through from her ankle. He quickly moved to take her by the arm before she had time to refuse help – which she usually did. He suggested she come to his apartment right by the side of the park, there he would get some ice and some arnica to help with the pain and the swelling.

"Arnica" she repeated, "What's that?"

"It'll help with the swelling and the pain" he continued as he allowed her to put her weight on him. She was certainly glad of his help, as she clutched at his most welcome arm. She was surprised by the heat that radiated where she touched both his arm and his hand. Dismissing the thought almost as quickly as it had appeared, just as she always did, they made their way in silence. They walked slowly together as he directed her towards his apartment. She felt so comfortable with this stranger, yet this wasn't a normal feeling for Elizabeth. Neither was it *usual for her to be in a state of comfortable silence.*

Within minutes they had arrived and he guided her to an outside chair on the patio. He gently elevated her foot onto a nearby stool. She was grateful for his help and sat in silence, as he unlocked the door and went inside. He returned a few moments later with some tiny pills, ice, a cup of water and a bandage.

"Here, take one of these" as he handed her the bottle of arnica tablets. "You can take one every ten minutes and it will help". He knelt down and took her swollen ankle into his hands. Once more the heat that radiated from his palm was unbelievable. He gently wrapped the ankle in the ice and asked how she was feeling. She was startled and it took her a moment to catch her breathe. The pain had almost gone and as he placed her ankle back onto the footstool she managed a weak "Thank You."

"Would you like a cup of tea or coffee?" He asked. She was still in a state of shock, not just because of the fall, but rather the sense of overwhelming comfortability she felt.

"Ummm, yes, yes please" she muttered.

“Which would you like, tea, coffee or herbal tea if you wish. I popped the kettle on earlier so it’s just boiled now. You’re welcome to stay as long as you need.” His kindly voice was making her feel more at ease now.

“Tea would be lovely” she replied, as she was still trying to take in the mornings events; not to mention those of the previous night too.

A cuckoo clock sounded in the kitchen and she was awakened from her trance-like thoughts. When he returned with a steaming hot cuppa, she admired the china crockery. She recognized the make and said “Thank You” once again without thinking.

“You’ve had quite a fall, though its soft tissue damage, it’ll ease if you continue to take the arnica at least hourly over the next couple of days” he advised.

“What’s arnica?” she questioned. As he looked into her face she felt she recognised him, there was definitely something familiar about him. Had she seen him in the park before? After all, usually she was out and about so early that very few people were there in the park and this had suited her.

“Arnica is a Homeopathic remedy to help with bruising, swelling and shock. It’s a little bit of magic in a bottle. I’ve used it for many years” he explained.

“I was just about to make myself some breakfast. Have you eaten, or would you at least like something to eat, even a piece of fruit, a slice of toast or a toasted currant teacake?” He really was a kindly man she thought.

"Ummm, what are you having?" she enquired.

"Well, I usually have some fresh fruit salad, maybe a teacake, though I can soon rustle up something, eggs, Greek yoghurt, muesli...?" He looked across at her as she looked so vulnerable.

He had spotted her so often in the park. She was always listening to something on her headphones and always seemed to be a million miles away. She always wore 'perfect' make-up and matching jogging outfits. Today this young lady was definitely out of sorts. His thoughts returned when she answered,

"Fresh fruit salad would be so lovely please." Elizabeth had surprised herself by first allowing him to assist her, then sitting in a stranger's garden, drinking tea and now was she really going to sit and eat with him? What was she doing? Accepting help from anyone was out of her normal comfort zone completely; not to mention that of a complete stranger.

In all the months she had been going for her morning run, she had never even said 'Hello' or 'Good Morning' to anyone. If anyone started to speak to her, she just ignored them and smiled a fake kind of smile. After all, that was normal wasn't it?

She sat in her thoughts a little longer, what was normal after all? *'A fake kind of smile'* rang through her ears as she recalled Robert's *fake* kind of smile last night at the party.

"Fake, fake, fake" she whispered.

"Are you ok?" the man asked, "did you say something?"

"Oh, ummm, no, ummmm, thank you" she said and she started to cry. In silence, he passed her a tissue. She smiled a sincere smile and looked up into those deep brown, soul searching eyes. They sat in further silence for a few more moments and he seemed to just accept that she was upset. He didn't probe, neither did he approach her to pop an arm around her, nor to hold her hand. She always expected someone to comfort her with physical touch whenever she cried. To be honest they were, on previous occasions predominantly 'crocodile tears,' and *fake moments.*

How long she sat there with him in a *totally comfortable silence* she was unaware. He just sipped his tea and sat patiently waiting to serve the fresh fruit salad. She became aware of other sounds nearby; they were after all, so close to the park. She could hear children talking and laughing, a man whistling and the sound of birds singing. It was as though they were welcoming in the fresh morning air and the sunshine.

The tears continued to flow, although there was no effort there at all. She just sat quietly with them, as he continued to pass more fresh tissues over the table. *Never* had she allowed a stranger to see her cry before. Yet, inside herself she knew she felt safe and felt as though she was wrapped in a protective bubble. She realised that she actually felt light round her and once more was surprised at how comfy she was. Although she was sat so close to the park in this private garden, it was as though they were within their own portal of safety. A feeling of nurturing surrounded her. *These feelings of comfort were so new to her and refreshing too.*

At her parent's home they always sat properly, sat up straight, rarely smiled, or laughed, or spoke *unless prompted.* She had always believed that that was the way it was. Here she was slumped in a chair, looking rough and raw without make-up, her hair was untidy from the fall and she was totally unladylike as she sat with one ankle on another chair.....and*, to top it all off,* she was crying in front of a stranger!

The tears stopped and he handed her the tea which was cool by now. How long had they sat there for? Weird she thought. As she sipped the tea, he looked across and returned into the kitchen. She could hear the kettle boil, as he shouted through that he was making a fresh brew.

"Thank you" she could barely whisper. The cuckoo clock rang out again. Surely they hadn't been here for an hour? He returned with a fresh teapot, cups and saucers. He poured in silence as she managed a smile. She realised that this was *a real smile.*

"Glad you're feeling better" he said as he removed the used cups and returned to the kitchen. She felt lighter and brighter somehow.

"Breakfast?" he asked.

"Yes please." as he passed her a bowl of fresh fruit salad and a pot of Greek yoghurt over.

"Thank you for your kindness" she said. She surprised herself with how genuine her appreciation was and how genuine this man was too.

As she looked across at him, she could see what looked like a heat haze around his head, almost like catching slight of dust particles as they fall on a hot summers' day. She wondered if she was in a dream, or had she banged her head, rather than her ankle?

They chatted easily about the park and the wildlife over breakfast and he asked how her ankle was feeling.

"The pain has almost gone to be honest. It certainly feels much, much better. You've been very kind and I have taken up so much of your time" She explained.

"It's a pleasure to help a maiden in distress" he said. If only he knew just how much her whole life was in distress, not just her ankle! She thought. Or did he? There was a look of deep knowing in his eyes and a certain feeling around him too.

"I'm retired so it's nice to have company," he interrupted her thoughts.

"The fruit salad was lovely and just what I needed," she answered.

"Would you like anything else?" He asked.

"No, but thank you so much" Elizabeth found herself looking into his eyes once more. They were so genuine and filled with kindness. She knew there was no hidden agenda or messages here. This was purely an act of immense kindness.

The breakfast crockery and cutlery were all cleaned away and he asked,

"Are you looking forward to the day ahead, do you have many plans?"

"Yes," she replied as he awakened her from her secret thoughts, where she was enjoying peace and tranquillity.

"I have twin sons who I need to collect at 4pm."

"I'll bet they've missed you?" he enquired. She simply smiled a smile, whilst knowing that that was unlikely. They seemed always to prefer being with their paternal grandmother or their father, rather than her.

As a sad look crossed over her face, she lowered her eyes, so that he couldn't see the tears.

"Children just need to be nurtured and listened to, they just want to grow up feeling loved and wanted" he continued. He spoke very gently and yet with an air of authority and dignity. She sensed he would be a great father and a wonderful grandfather too. Her thoughts drifted to her own grandfather who often used to say 'Little girls should be seen and not heard'.

Her eyes welled up once again and she felt his gaze upon her, though with complete compassion. Why was she feeling so utterly weird? It was as if the floodgates for her emotions had been leaking. Now fully opened, letting all these feelings finally be heard and acknowledged. In truth, floodgates or not, she had no idea what, or how, to deal with them. It was as though they had opened upon a desert, rather than landing on a wooded area of land, where the water could adhere and be utilised, soaked up by the tree roots. Instead, the water was moving so quickly, it was shifting the sand itself. She felt as though she would get washed away at any moment. It felt like an internal tsunami.

"The sands of time" he stated. "Had he been in her head? What on earth made him say that?

"All things change with the sands of time. Time changes all things."

"Would you like me to help you to stand up. Let's see if you can put pressure on that ankle now?" he asked.

"I've seen you many times before, so I'm guessing you're local, though I'll happily drive you if needs be."

As she listened to his kind words, her heart seemed to skip a beat. Not because she was having a heart attack, nor because it was on any level in a romantic sense; it just simply was. *Was it something to do with the floodgates opening she wondered?*

As he held out his arm to assist her she gladly took it. She'd been unaware of her foot and ankle as the pain had subsided. She had continued to take the arnica when he had prompted her and now as she stood up, she realised that although yes, there was certainly a distinctive twinge, it felt so much easier and she was more than happy to walk home. She was surprised because it also felt warm, just as it had when he had first placed his hands around it earlier that morning.

"There, you seem okay, how does it feel?" he enquired.

"Really wonderful to be honest, considering how painful and swollen it was, just over an hour ago" Elizabeth's delight was evident in her tone of voice.

"Do you feel okay to walk or would you rather I take you home?" he asked with genuine compassion in his voice.

"I'll walk and I'll actually enjoy the park whilst I do, I can't believe how much I've been missing whilst I've always had my headphones and phone with me. Thank you for all your care and attention, not to mention the lovely breakfast, I feel amazing. "

"Please feel free to pop in again if you like, whenever you are passing" he suggested and she knew she had an open invitation anytime. He lived very close to the park, so she knew she could easily find the house again. Besides she felt she had quite a treat.

"Let me know how it heals, keep taking the arnica and look after yourself," he suggested as she was about to leave through the gate.

"Thank you so much for your kindness, thank you. It was wonderful to meet you too and I'm sure we will meet again, sooner, rather than later" she offered. She realised she rarely said 'Thank you' and very rarely meant it when she did. She was surprised at her openness.

She truly wasn't sure whether to shake his hand or just nod and acknowledge her appreciation. He smiled as they stood together by the gate.

"You can have a hug if you prefer?" he suggested.

"Thank you. I've only just realised that I haven't asked your name".

"Alexander and it has been a pleasure to meet you" he stated whilst they enjoyed their hug.

"I'm Elizabeth and most grateful for your help and kindness. Thank you once again."

She was surprised at the ease of this hug. Was it because he was old? Never before had she been hugged with nothing other than affection and kindness. There was no hidden agenda here, just simplicity. Despite the intimacy she had shared with her husband and subsequent boyfriends, this was a hug to knock the socks off all others. *Being held with nothing other than love was LOVE itself.* 'Wow' she thought.

They parted and she waved as she walked to the corner. She felt so different, lighter and brighter and realised that as people passed they were smiling at her. It was then that she realised that she too was smiling. Wow indeed, so many new experiences in just one single day and the day was just beginning.

The walk was only about twenty minutes and though she had a slight limp she managed quite easily to make the journey. As she walked her thoughts drifted to the previous evenings' events, the argument, the fight and her sons. The words *'Children just need to be loved and nurtured'* echoed around in her head. *Nurtured* was a word that she had rarely heard. What exactly did it mean?

Chapter Three

Nurturing the definition of "……nourish, rear, bring up." The words kept repeating over and over in her mind. Was she nurturing her sons? If she didn't know what it meant, how could she nurture them? She was certainly aware that they preferred being with their father or her ex mother in law rather than with her. Did they nurture the boys?

She sat down quietly with a cup of hot chocolate. She reflected upon all the activities that she had ever done with her sons. She took them to the play area where they could play in the ball pond or slide, whilst she waited for them. Yet, as the tears began to well inside her 'Yes' she admitted to herself, that she had never actually played with them. She never really listened to what they wanted to do when they had often asked to go to the local park or the swimming baths. She had always made some excuse and in truth, she really just wanted to gossip to her friends on the phone or follow things on Facebook.

She began to wonder and consider what her twins really thought of her. What did anyone think of her? What did she think of herself? The thoughts hit her like a hammer coming down on a nail at great speed. What had she been doing with her life? She didn't have to work thank goodness, as her ex-husband paid more than adequate maintenance; but what was she doing with her life? Was she happy? She had previously thought she was after all. There were so many questions. Would she ever find the answers she wondered?

Looking up at the clock she realised that a full hour had slipped away. She needed to get showered and dressed in order to be presentable for her sons. She didn't have much time now before having to leave to collect them.

As she washed and bathed in the shower she looked around her at all the products, the shampoo, conditioner, two in one shampoos and the shower gels, creams, face wash, spot creams.....she felt weird, as though she had awakened from a deep sleep. Were these really all necessary?

As she washed, she noticed the swelling had greatly reduced on her ankle and standing on it really was getting easier by the minute. She felt a sense of deep gratitude sweep through her at the simplicity of life and *suddenly realised how complicated she had made it.*

Once more tears rolled down her cheeks and she felt an ache and a pain in her heart like never before. As the shampoo bubbles made their own circles as they travelled down the plug hole, she looked on aware for the first time in her life, of how much her life had seemed to simply be going down the proverbial plughole. Tears and sobs filled the bathroom and once again the pain in her heart increased.

She lay on the bed wrapped in a damp towel for quite some time, thinking of just where she would start to bring about these necessary changes of listening more, considering others and starting life with a new outlook.

Automatically she reached for her phone and there it was right on the bedside cabinet. She knew it hadn't been there earlier and began to wonder at the strangeness of this day. There were no messages, so she simply text her ex-mother-in-law to let her know that she would be there soon to collect the twins. In the text, she asked how she was and hoped that the boys had behaved and that they had also enjoyed themselves whilst with her. She also said a *"Thank You"* to her, for having the boys and said that she looked forwards to seeing her later.

As she re-read through the text she had just written, she wondered why she had never offered any words of kindness to her before. She had always referred to 'her' as the 'Witch-Bitch,' mother-in-law or rather, ex mother-in-law. She realised how much unkindness she had given to others and obviously to herself! Once again the tears started and she looked in the mirror. She automatically moved as if to clean up the mascara, and yet, when she saw her reflection, she wasn't wearing mascara and hadn't put on any make-up at all. The words *'No more masks'* echoed in her head as she popped her mobile in her handbag.

Chapter Four

Travelling to collect the twins was a joy. She eased the Range Rover into the driveway and felt comforted by the familiar sound of the gravel under the tyres. She was aware that she was looking forwards to seeing them both. She usually dreaded picking them up and often found them a chore and a bore. Today was really proving to be different and was truly beginning to be quite a revelation too.

The front door was already ajar as she entered the house. The smell of fresh flowers greeted her; both lilies and roses. As she looked at them in the vase, it seemed as if the colours were more vibrant than ever before. She could hear familiar voices in the lounge and as she listened she could also feel the comfortability from her children. Usually when they were with her, they were stressed and noisy.

As she listened, she could hear them say they didn't want to go home to mummy, they wanted to stay and have fun with Grandma.

"Mummy never listens to us and is always distracted by her new boyfriend, or the TV or usually her phone." They were freely expressing their anger at not being heard. Tears fell, as she listened to their heartfelt criticisms. "I miss Grandad" said Will

"He was always so kind to us and gave us lots of cuddles. He took us to the park to play on the model trains. *Mummy never does that".*

"Mummy will be here soon" said Grandma and both boys let out a huge groan.

"Now come on boys, remember she's your Mummy and she loves you dearly. Be kind and patient with her, you're really quite a handful at times" Sheila continued.

"She doesn't like us" they stated and as she listened in the hallway the cat brushed past her and meowed.

"Oh listen, perhaps your mother is here already," said Sheila.

"Let's go and see and you boys be as good as gold. Remember what I told you about being kind to her."

Elizabeth was stood crying in the hallway. Sheila put her arm around her and led her into the kitchen, sitting her down at the huge oak dining table.

"I'll pop the kettle on, would you like tea or coffee Elizabeth."

"Right boys, now you two go upstairs and get your things, whilst Mummy and I have a few quiet minutes. Then please go into the garden and play on the slide...I'll be along shortly if you'd like me to push you on the swings."

As the two women sat in the kitchen, Elizabeth noticed the fresh flower arrangements and how homely the kitchen felt. Usually she hated coming here and she rarely stayed for more than five minutes. She barely exchanged pleasantries and small talk about the boys and what they had been doing.

She sipped her cuppa whilst Sheila just held her other hand. She made no attempt to coax Elizabeth into conversation. Sheila just wanted this younger woman to feel comfortable. Elizabeth was extremely grateful to her for her patience and obvious genuine concern. For the second time that day, she was experiencing a comfortable silence; whereas normally she hated silence with a vengeance.

The tea tasted different and she began to *realise just how different she was feeling too.* She placed the cup down and for the first time ever, placed her other hand over that of Sheila's as a gesture of her thanks and sincere gratitude. Without thinking, she looked in to her mother-in-law's eyes and felt complete peace and compassion.

Elizabeth had never experienced such inner peace and had rarely looked so deeply into someone else's eyes; unless it was a boyfriend. She had searched for such a love and yet here it was, complete and total unconditional love. There was no need for words as they just sat together, although it was inevitable that eventually the twins would require attention.

Sure enough, within a few minutes they wandered inside the kitchen, requesting a drink. Sheila arose and poured out two glasses of fresh elderflower cordial. She asked if they would like some ice too. Neither of her sons acknowledged her presence in the room. She continued to watch as they downed the fresh juice and wandered outside again, without uttering a single word to her. Sheila had simply poured them a drink and offered them refreshments without making a fuss. She heard the word *'reflect'* clearly in her mind again. She remembered that each and every time the boys requested a drink or a meal or her attention, she felt it was such a huge effort and *usually told them so.* Yet, here she was realizing that everything could in fact be completely effortless and simple. *Why had she always made everything into a drama?*

As if reading her mind, Sheila placed a hand on Elizabeth's shoulder and guided her into the garden. It was just coming up to 5pm and Sheila knew the boys would be feeling hungry anytime soon. Oblivious to the time, Elizabeth was startled, when Sheila suggested she prepare a meal for them all. She asked with loving kindness if she too would like to stay.

The answer "Yes" was uttered before Elizabeth even thought about her answer. Sheila just poured her a glass of elderflower, whilst she began preparing some healthy salad and potato wedges with fresh rosemary from the herb garden. Elizabeth felt unable to move, as she watched Sheila simply get on with the kitchen chores.

The boys arrived once again after a few minutes they made a drama about feeling that they were starving and thirsty again. Sheila reassured them that they were staying here for the evening meal with both her and mummy.

"With mummy," they both remarked in unison.

"She always just wants to leave and orders us about in the car on the way home," they stated as if Elizabeth were a million miles away, certainly not sat within several feet of them.

"Now boys, I've told you to be kinder to your mother and behave for her. I'll shout you as soon as this is ready, it'll be about thirty minutes. You can have an apple or a pear, if you're really starving."

Once again Elizabeth sat in tears across the table. What had she been doing with her life? Her sons and the way she had treated her mother-in-law previously was truly appalling. Once more she felt a strange pain in her heart, as though she was having a heart attack.

As she reached for her chest and gasped for air, Sheila simply stated that her heart centre was being opened.

"It's at least the third time today that this has happened," Elizabeth spoke in a very quiet voice.

"You are opening up to compassion and forgiveness." Sheila simply explained.

"What does that mean?" queried Elizabeth.

Sheila smiled a huge smile of reassurance and Elizabeth felt a calmness go right through her body.

"We will get the little men fed and then I'll explain more fully after we have eaten. You are all more than welcome to stay here with me this evening, though if you prefer, I'll keep them another night. You can go home and collect them tomorrow? They are tired out, as they've played outdoors most of the day and we visited the baby animal zoo earlier. So after eating, they can watch a little T.V. then have a nice bath and then go to bed. I washed and dried their pyjamas earlier, so they are fine for this evening and I have plenty of spare clothes for them for tomorrow too. I'd quite enjoy some female company after having the boys all weekend. If that's okay with you of course?" Sheila enquired.

Elizabeth nodded sheepishly, as she continued to allow the soft tears to fall. Sheila passed her more tissues and asked if salad, potato wedges and salmon were appealing enough for her evening meal. She simply nodded once again in silence, as the volume of her tears increased.

Chapter Five

The meal tasted like one of the very best that she had ever ingested. The simplicity of potato wedges, salad and salmon was so tasty.

"It's cooked with love" Sheila said and knowing that Elizabeth was in shock at the day's happenings, she simply took the boys upstairs for their evening bath. Elizabeth was just sat listening to their laughter and, for the first time possibly ever, feeling *the love between Sheila and her grandsons*. Had it always been there? Had she realised before and not acknowledged it or was this truly the first time she had noticed? Where had she been?

As she thought about the days' events and the previous evening's events, she realised that she had not thought about Robert all day. She had not even looked at her phone for hours. Elizabeth had convinced herself that she loved Robert, that he was in love with her and that she was in love with him. She wondered now just what love is or was. Someone had once said to her that *'she was in love with being in love'*. Now she was really questioning everything that she had previously believed love to be.

Sheila had made her a lovely cup of hot lemon and honey and ordered her, in the kindest of ways, to stay in the comfy chair in the lounge. She suggested that she should stay here for the night, though it was to be her decision. The boys came downstairs to say 'Goodnight' after their bath and as she kissed them gently, she looked at how beautiful their features were. They were identical twins, though to her they had distinctive differences and certainly different personalities too. They looked predominantly like their father which, after the divorce she had found increasingly difficult to acknowledge. They reminded her so much of him. They did have her dark hair and dark features though and, for the first time, she smiled as she recognised Ted's cheeky grin and the warmth in their eyes; just like their father.

Seconds later they dashed upstairs to their beloved Grandma. As she listened the boys grew quieter, as Sheila had started to read them a bedtime story. She had enjoyed listening to their laughter during their bath. The moans and groans of the saga of them both having to put on their pyjamas and their subsequent arguing about wanting to stay up a while longer too. Now she was content simply to listen to the sound of silence.

'Silence and reflections' she heard whispered in her right ear. *'Enjoy the silence and reflections, learn from them and grow.'* Once again the feeling in her heart centre was that of pain and discomfort, just as it had been previously during the day.

Several minutes later she could hear Sheila coming down the stairs. She popped her head around the lounge door to ask if Elizabeth would like anything else. She explained that the boys were already fast asleep and tucked up for the night.

"I'll just pop the kettle on and make myself a brew" Sheila informed Elizabeth.

"If you would like a bath you are more than welcome. I have some lovely bath salts and aromatherapy oils, which you are welcome to use."

Elizabeth felt like she had been wrapped in a bubble; just as she had earlier in the day with the Mediterranean chap, Alexander. She had been treated with such kindness by a complete stranger. Now she was enjoying so much more kindness from her ex mother-in-law, whom she had previously referred to as 'The Witch Bitch.' How could she have been so cruel and have misunderstood all this kindness? Her mother-in-law had always been odd, though had never ever, been nasty with her.

Elizabeth thought back to her own mother and father who would be sitting at home watching T.V. or maybe out at a social gathering in the local community. They were always so supportive of the local village and keen to organise events and engage with others. She tried to think of a time when she had been treated with such kindness from them and offered a bath and a sleep over. How strange indeed she pondered, as Sheila entered the room and interrupted her thoughts.

"How are you feeling now Elizabeth?" she asked.

"Do you feel tired? How's your heart centre feeling?" "I feel a little tired yes and I might just take you up on that offer of a bath, if that's okay. The aromatherapy oils sound inviting and I feel that some T.L.C. might not go amiss to be honest. It's been quite a day, all in all." Elizabeth replied

"Use the bath in my en-suite and then if you want to use the jets to massage you, the boys won't be disturbed at all. Though I'm sure that they would sleep through a hurricane to be honest. There's some fresh linen in the cupboard, you might recall staying when you and Ted were married? There is a spare dressing gown in there too. I'm sure we can find you a spare nightie, or pyjamas if you prefer? Would you like me to show you up there or will you remember?"

"Thank you, yes please," Elizabeth replied with a deepening sense of humility and gratitude. The two of them walked up the beautiful open staircase and onto the landing before moving into the Master bedroom. The fresh smell of flowers from the vase of lilies was so lovely. Elizabeth was so grateful to be treated with such generosity. Sheila showed her around and advised her to pop the oils in once she was in that bath and to be aware that they might cause her feet to soften, potentially maybe becoming slippery on the tiles. As the towels, dressing gown and night-wear were laid upon the chair, Elizabeth expressed her thanks and stated she wouldn't be too long. Sheila nodded and smiled a knowing smile before leaving the room.

Chapter Six

As she lay in the bath, Elizabeth let the stresses and strains of the day ebb away. She felt that the oils eased her emotions away and she didn't feel she needed the jets too. To be honest, she thought to herself, *she was enjoying the silence*. This was certainly a new concept. Her thoughts drifted, as she remembered staying here whilst her father-in-law had been poorly and Sheila was backwards and forwards from the hospice. Elizabeth had never felt comfortable talking about William and even thinking about his imminent death. Sheila however mentioned him regularly, especially to the boys. They innocently accepted that he had simply gone to the angels and always looked over them from heaven.

She thought of Ted, her ex-husband and wondered what it would feel like to lose a father. William had certainly been a wonderful, loving and hands-on father. He was a very creative and practical man. She recalled Ted mentioning him with great affection and warmth, as he remembered him mending his bicycle and helping him choose his first car and motorbike. As her thoughts lingered on Ted, she realised that she was smiling a huge smile. She thought of the time they had shared this huge tub together and made love slowly and passionately. The smile remained and yet the tears returned. She just let them fall and allowed these emotions to surface, just like the bubbles in the water.

Time passed quickly though she realised that she was cool, rather than cold. Her skin was beginning to look like a prune. As she dried her body and put on the dressing gown, once again she felt like she was wrapped in a bubble. Emptying the bath and washing away the last of the suds and the oils, she felt a hand upon her right shoulder.

She felt calm and although she was usually freaked out and startled by such things. This time she reached towards her shoulder, as though to place her hand over that of the other person. She realised there was no physical hand there and just accepted what she had experienced. The whole day had been such a peculiar one anyway.

Tired and weary, yet both relaxed and peaceful, she descended the oak staircase. The beauty and the feel of the wood had eluded her previously and she couldn't believe how beautiful this house truly was. Why on earth had she never noticed before? The carpet beneath her feet was so soft and comfortable and the pictures and wall hangings so elegant and stylish. The oak door frames stood out, as if they were still part of a sacred tree or a forest. In fact, she realised that the whole house itself seemed to feel an at-oneness and deep peace.

She moved gracefully into the lounge to sit comfortably in the lounger once more and thanked Sheila for her hospitality.

"Did you enjoy your bath, you look peaceful," Sheila smiled a knowing smile and asked her in a very gentle manner.

"Oh yes, very much" smiled back Elizabeth.

She gave Sheila a huge smile and there was a radiance of deep gratitude from her eyes. As the two women sat easily with one another a most comfortable silence seemed to envelope, not just them, but the whole room too. Putting down the novel she was reading, Sheila approached Elizabeth placing a gentle hand upon her shoulder.

"Would you like a hot drink Elizabeth, perhaps a Horlicks or an Ovaltine, tea, coffee or herbal tea, maybe even a hot chocolate?"

"Yes please" she answered and was happy just to sit quietly, listening to the nothing-ness of the house. Parts of the house were almost two hundred years old. Sheila and William had acquired it long before she and Ted met, so it had been familiar to her for many years. Here she was staying here without Ted and she was enjoying herself. The house was set in its own grounds and in beautiful mature gardens, which Sheila obviously cherished.

As Sheila busied herself in the kitchen, Elizabeth could hear her humming to herself and felt herself sinking deeper into the lounger. Never before had she been more relaxed. The sound of the telephone in the hallway made her jump although Sheila answered it quickly. As she chatted to her friend Annie, Elizabeth could hear Sheila making arrangements for the following morning. She mentioned she had the boys staying and that Elizabeth was here too. They were just about to share a cuppa and she would ask if the extended family would also like to join them tomorrow. From the tone of Sheila's voice, it was obvious that genuine affection was abound. As Elizabeth listened the now familiar feeling that her heart was hurting came over her once again.

Laying down the two cups on the side tables, Sheila noticed that Elizabeth was once again clutching her heart centre.

"It is bothering you again honey" Sheila enquired.

"Yes, though I feel I must be getting more used to it now. It's certainly not as painful, nor uncomfortable as it has been throughout the day."

"You'll get more used to it over the next few days, it will ease as it gets stronger."

Sheila didn't push Elizabeth for a reply, she simply waited.

"What does it mean when you say the heart centre is opening up?"

Sheila looked Elizabeth straight in the eyes and explained that the heart has its own intelligence. She continued to explain that most people only ever think from within their heads, rather than from their hearts. The heart allows intuition, insight, trust, wisdom and a deepening of our natural discernment. When we live from the head, we *think thoughts, rather than feel what is right for us.* Animals have unconditional love and amazing intuition, just as the ancient civilizations did. She continued to explain that due to modern technology, mobile phones, televisions, laptops, iPads, radios and the like, that very few people enjoyed or even experienced silence; therefore people would all too often resist, or dismiss those innate feelings.

Elizabeth continued to listen and was becoming inspired and engrossed in the conversation. She was surprised at just how simple Sheila explained it all and that it all made perfect sense. Sheila paused, as if checking that Elizabeth was following her conversation and was able to comprehend. She had explained this concept many times to people previously, finding it best to explain with frequent pauses and patience.

Sheila had always been very sensitive to people's emotions, atmospheres in houses and rooms, especially perhaps after a row or an argument. She had often seen colours around people, animals and trees, and, though only a child at that time, she had endlessly searched as she got older for what all these things meant. As she continued to share her insights with Elizabeth, she was aware not to overwhelm her. This lady was fragile and tired, after a busy day of what was called in the spiritual world *awakenings, experiences and connections to her heart and soul.* She knew there would no doubt be plenty of further questions and there was plenty of time to share these wisdoms another day.

Sheila's voice seemed hypnotic to Elizabeth and as they drank the Chamomile tea, she realised just how tired she was. Without a word, Elizabeth knew that Sheila realised she was fading fast and getting ready for the land of zzzz's.

"Would you like me to come up with you?" Sheila asked,

"I won't be long behind you myself," she stated.

"I'm okay and thank you so much for your kindness" Elizabeth replied.

"Feel free to have a lie in if you wish in the morning. I'm always an early bird, so I'll be up and about when the boys wake up. We have been invited out with Annie tomorrow and you are more than welcome to come, although we can of course discuss it tomorrow, as I know you are shattered. Goodnight and God bless."

The two women shared a genuine smile with one another as Elizabeth made ready for bed. Placing her empty mug in the kitchen, she looked around at how tidy and homely this beautiful place seemed. Once more she felt the now familiar hand upon her *right shoulder,* as it seemed to gently guide her upstairs.

Brushing her teeth and settling herself, Elizabeth felt a huge surge of peace throughout her body. She curled herself into the huge Grandmother bed and noticed Sheila had placed a teddy bear on the other pillow. She reached over happily, pulling the teddy into her chest. She breathed out a breath of surrender, as she drifted off in to what was to be another one of the deepest sleeps that she had ever experienced.

Chapter Seven

Waking up the following morning to the sound of the boy's laughter as they played in the garden, Elizabeth stirred. She was once again surprised at just how comfortable she felt having stayed over with her ex mother-in-law. So much had happened in the last day and a half. She felt so different and at peace with herself. As she sat up on the huge pillows, she reflected upon the previous day and the kindly gentleman she had met in the park, who helped her with her sprained ankle. She poked the said ankle from beneath the covers. It was black and blue from the fall and yet wasn't painful at all, as she moved it from side to side, she tried to recall his name and wondered whether she had asked what it was. She knew where he lived and she *'knew'* she would see him again.

The sound of the boy's laughter broke into her thoughts, as she looked around the huge bedroom. She opened the curtains to take in the magnificent view of the garden's splendour. Opening the windows to the sound of the birds and the leaves gently blowing in the breeze, she looked out and over into the surrounding fields. She could see the farmer and his trusty tractor quite a way away.

Elizabeth had always loved the city and thought that country folk were all ignorant bumpkins. My, how her attitudes and views were changing she thought. The boys caught a glimpse of her as she stood in the huge bay window. They smiled at her and motioned to her to come and join them. How strange it was when Elizabeth thought back to her previous existence, as normally she dreaded starting the day with them, normally she would have them breakfasted, dressed and off to the adventure play park so she could rest up. If Ted was collecting them, then she would be delighted to get rid of them and have some peace. Here she was, looking forwards to going downstairs and spending time with her sons.

Wrapping herself in the lovely soft towelling robe, she slipped on some slippers and descended the staircase. Once more she admired the furnishings, all of which she had previously ignored. The smell of fresh bread and coffee filled the air. Elizabeth felt so at ease with herself. As she neared the kitchen, she realised that normally she was dressed and covered with make-up and a variety of products, without which she felt had vulnerable and uncomfortable. Yet, here she was in a simple nightdress and dressing gown.

Being greeted with a loving smile and warm hug from Sheila was so natural, as she entered the kitchen. When she was asked how she had slept, all seemed to be so simple that it was almost dreamlike.

"What would you like for breakfast Elizabeth? I have made some fresh rolls and bread too so you are welcome to have some toast. I also have crumpets and jam. I'm happy to make you some fresh eggs from the chickens or a fruit smoothie, fresh fruit salad and whatever else. I usually have bacon in the fridge for when Ted comes – he still loves his bacon butty with HP sauce. Kettle's on and the boys were starving when they came down, so they've already been fed and watered."

The patio doors were open and Elizabeth could see the boys playing football on the lawn. They had obviously collected the fresh eggs from the chicken shed, as the basket was left at the side of the door. They had always said they loved that particular job first thing in the morning when they stayed here.

Her thoughts drifted to her own childhood and what she had enjoyed doing as a little girl. Her own grandparents were very old when she was younger, so she had rarely enjoyed quality time with them. They had always seemed grumpy and crotchety. She had always known to sit quietly and behave.

The boys were laughing hysterically about something and both women moved to the patio doorway to see what was amusing them so much. The huge fishpond was one of their favourite places to watch the fish and a frog kept slipping from the edge of the pond back into the water. The fountain poured water into the middle and the fish seemed oblivious to the antics of the frog, who was by now becoming exhausted at his failed attempts to return to the garden. Sheila reached for the fishing net and gently stretched over, scooping up the frog and placing him on the grass. He hopped off into the undergrowth as they all watched on.

Will was hugging Elizabeth's waist as they watched. Never before had she experienced such genuine affection from either of her sons. It was as though they had naturally intuited the difference in their mother. She had wondered the previous evening whilst she enjoyed her bath, how she would approach them both and sit with them to explain how truly sorry she was that she had failed to recognise how wonderful it truly was to share time with them, maybe they had intuited her thoughts?

Tears ran down her cheeks in silence, as she felt the loving connection between them both. It was then that she also realised Benjamin was holding her hand tightly too. With Will to her right and Ben to her left, she felt so secure and totally loved. Will let go of her waist and held her other hand. The boys guided her to their secret den. They had often told her about it and yet never had she asked, or enquired about how it was built, or what they liked to do in there. They explained Grandad William had made it for them before he was poorly, in fact whilst she was pregnant, and they loved it.

As they showed her inside, it was a small version of a log cabin with a desk and simple chairs made 'from wood from a ship wreck' Granddad had said. They had colouring pencils and paints, a blackboard and an easel, bricks and a little workbench too with various tools; hammers and screwdrivers, etc. They had bean bags and cushions on the floor and there were a variety of books on the shelves.

"Daddy loves it in here with us and shows us how to make wooden toys. Grandad left us lots of photographs of the toys he made for the children in the village. Look."

Elizabeth was amazed to see a leather-bound photo album filled with hand-made wooden dolls, cots, rattles, toy trains and a huge array of toys; both small and large that William had made during his life. They obviously loved it and seemed to feel so close to their late Grandfather. She was so touched and delighted, as they continued to show her the most minute details of the place they loved to call their den. He had carved lots of tiny animals, insects and birds into the furniture and on the walls too. The effort that he had so obviously put in here for his grandchildren to enjoy was so evident.

"Do you like it Mummy" they asked with so much enthusiasm.

"I love it to be honest and I'm so sorry that I have never asked you to bring me in here before. It's really very lovely indeed" she replied. Her heart was filled with humility and peace, together with love. Now at last, she had an understanding of why it was that they still chatted about their grandfather. His presence was here and it was so tangible. The whole place had a soul all of its own and she could feel it. Why had she found it so hard to comprehend and even accept death before this moment? Why she had previously not understood this she failed to comprehend. Her thoughts wondered to her childhood as she searched for what seemed to be the missing link.

"Why don't you go and have some brekkie with Grandma and then come back and play with us. Then we can show you the tree house too if you like?"

"I'd really like that very much" Elizabeth answered and was filled with awe at the innocence and forgiveness her sons showed her. They never questioned why she had failed to show them any particular interest or attention, they simply accepted that things had now changed and moved on. The past was the past. That was where it belonged. The present was right here, right now and they clearly intended to make the most of their precious day. The delight that they had her undivided attention was so obvious. *They were totally living in the moment*. She was clearly moved and touched by what was, in essence, still only the beginning of the day. She wondered what would happen in the coming hours.

Chapter Eight

They all walked into the kitchen where Sheila was busy preparing vegetables for lunch and laughing to herself. She was listening to the local radio station and was totally unaware of their presence. Ben approached her from behind and popped his hand upon her small waist.

"Grandma, mum has just been in our den and she liked it. She said she would like to see the tree house later too! Today is going to be a great day and very special. I can feel it Grandma. What are we doing today? Are you coming to play with us?" His excitement was barely containable and it was so evident that the twins had missed their mothers' participation in their childhood up until now.

Sheila looked over at Elizabeth who was smiling down at her sons with such a look of peace on her face and yet gentle tears in her eyes. A knowing look passed between them when Elizabeth looked up and, without words, so much understanding and compassion was shared.

"I've just popped some fruit salad and yoghurt there for you Elizabeth. If you like I'll put some toast in the toaster too?"

The boys had already disappeared back into the garden and their laughter could clearly be heard over the noise of the chickens and the other birds. As Elizabeth stood up as if to see what was going on, Sheila explained that the local cat would have just got too close and the boys were quite used to shooing him off.

"Poor bugger, he tries his luck every day and fails miserably. Honestly you would think he would know better by now."

Breakfast was lovely and as Elizabeth tucked in, she realised just how hungry she was. Sheila left her to eat whilst she prepared the vegetables and tidied the kitchen. Nothing seemed too much for her and seemingly nothing was a chore. The DJ on the radio was telling a joke and within seconds both women were howling. So much can be shared through the language of laughter and Elizabeth realised that she rarely laughed. As she continued to think about it, she had rarely ever smiled either.

Sheila reminded Elizabeth of the phone call the previous evening from Annie, regarding the invitation to a sound bath. Annie had mentioned that they were all welcome and Sheila had promised to call before 10am to confirm their arrangements either way.

"Do you have plans Elizabeth, you are of course welcome to attend with us, or I'll happily take the boys, so you can rest in the garden, or you could go home if you prefer. I'll happily drop the boys at yours later."

"What is a Sound Bath?" Elizabeth enquired?

"Well it really is something to be experienced to be honest Elizabeth. The boys have been before and loved it. They are often zonked when we get back and they sleep so peacefully for a couple of evenings after. In simple terms, the body is made up light, sound and energy. All sounds affect the body, some music is soothing, whereas other music is rather harsh." Elizabeth was listening intently as Sheila continued;

"Sounds can heal; the frequency of ultrasounds as you know, can break down gallstones, or kidney stones. The frequency of the sounds in the sound bath increase the vibration of the individual cells, thus encouraging the circulation of the blood and obviously the lymphatic system too. To be honest, I usually need to go to the loo frequently afterwards, as do many others. It's like having a deep cleanse I guess. Who knows, it's probably great for cancers too, as the vibration would probably break up the cells." Sheila continued to explain with great enthusiasm and Elizabeth continued to listen;

"Chanting is usually very soothing and can provide us with an overall feeling of calm and peace. A Sound Bath is when, in this case at least, Annie plays the gongs and the singing bowls, she also has chimes and a variety of Native American Indian flutes. Often people sit on the floor or lie down. I've been going for years and have introduced so many friends to them. All of them have loved it so much and some have even been inspired to train as a sound therapist."

Elizabeth was quite surprised that Sheila was obviously not a 'Witch Bitch' at all. She really had been so incredibly mean.

"There's no harm in trying," encouraged Sheila and Elizabeth realised that she rarely tried anything new – other than to impress in order that she be liked and accepted.

"It is the school holidays after all. I'd love to give it a go and if the twins enjoy themselves so much, it seems a shame not to attend." Elizabeth had agreed within seconds.

"Great, we have a plan then. I'll just phone her and confirm that we will be there for 11am, if that's okay with you. Lunch will be ready when we get back and we will see what the afternoon brings."

Whilst Sheila phoned Annie, Elizabeth pottered into the garden and looked around for her boys. They were happily playing in the sand pit and the football and cricket set were out on the lawn. She listened to them chat easily to one another saying they hoped Mum would let them go to see Annie as she usually had a treat for them. They were very clearly hopeful that Mum might attend too. Annie always invited them to play the instruments at the end of the session. They were both often left alone for a few minutes to make as much noise as they wanted.

Elizabeth's thoughts drifted to her own childhood. The words *'Little girls should be seen and not heard'* echoed through her mind, as she visualised her grandfather staring across at her, whenever she was playing in their garden. Never had she even imagined banging gongs and being allowed this extent of freedom. The comfortability that the boys so clearly showed whilst they were here was so touching, yet sad too, as she realised that when they were with her, they were stressed and demanding.

'Take the learnings from your reflections.' That now familiar voice was there again. She moved to sit on the beautiful hand carved bench that William had made only months before he passed away. She had never given it much thought or attention before, and yet as she ran her hands along the woodwork, she noticed for the very first time, the beauty of the intricate carvings of animals, birds and insects.

It was becoming clearly obvious to her that living with her mobile phone and all the technological items she had, clearly distracted her from living her life and enjoying peace and silence. As she sat quietly whilst the boys continued to play, she thought of how life had just been about moving, or rather stumbling, from one distraction to another. She had always tried to please others; mainly herself, friends and her boyfriends.

As her thoughts drifted to times gone by, she thought of Ted, the children's father and how little she had ever tried to please him. How he never demanded her attention and always seemed to be so comfortable in his own skin. She thought of how jealous she often became when he spoke to other women, and especially when she saw how comfortable he was with his mother.

Once again, her thoughts drifted to her own mother and how uncomfortable she was in her presence. *She was always trying to seek approval and acceptance from her.* Often she didn't even feel she was noticed, as her mother was always busy either organising things with the local villagers, or with the priest at church.

The now familiar pain crept into her heart centre again as she lightly gripped her chest. As the pain came and went, as it had done many times in the last day and a half, she realised how calm and peaceful she felt *right here and now, in this present moment.* She also recognised that she was feeling comfortable and at one with herself, even though she was dressed in a nightshirt, dressing gown and sat in the garden; *all without make-up! S*o much about her had changed this last day and a half. She was beginning to understand just how much repair work needed to be done. Just how much she had missed out on in life and for the very first time in her life, she was beginning to comprehend the words *'living in the moment.'*

Sheila approached her with a huge grin across her face and was clearly delighted to be taking Elizabeth with her.

"Annie lives near your apartment dear, so if you like, you can get dressed and even collect some of your things. It's an open invitation if you would like to stay with me for another day or so. Just a thought."

Nodding like one of the ornamental nodding Churchill dogs Elizabeth was clearly in agreement. She smiled to herself, as normally if that offer had been made, she would have just been glad for Sheila to have the boys. She herself would have simply just rested or ventured out shopping *alone*! Now she really wanted to get to know this lady to whom she had previously been so awful and to really begin to *'live in the moment,'* making up for so much lost time with her sons.

Chapter Nine

The boys could hardly contain their excitement, when they heard the news that Elizabeth had agreed to stay at Grandma's house with them for a few more days. They really missed her when they weren't with her, though felt that she never listened, nor understood, when they told her of their feelings.

They loved their mother and Grandma was always telling them to tell her that they did too. Grandma told them she loved them so often that sometimes they thought she was just a 'big softie.' Daddy always told them he loved them, even though it might only be in a phone conversation before bed. They thought of him often and they had dearly missed him in their everyday life since the divorce. However, whenever they spent time with him, they were thrilled and excited. He was always in the moment with them and loved sharing their fun in the den, or climbing trees in Grandma's garden. Grandma would shout at them for 'being so high and for frightening her half to death' as she would say! Dad would then roll his eyes into his head and when she wandered back into the house, or another part of the garden, they would laugh and usually end up actually crying with laughter between themselves.

Dad was happy to talk freely about Grandpa and answer any of their questions. They barely remembered him in truth, though always felt a warm, glowing, tingly feeling when he was mentioned. They knew he had been such a lovely man and sometimes when he was mentioned a tear or two would well up in their father's eyes.

"Will you miss us when we are dead?" Will was always the bolder of the two boys and so much more outspoken than Ben.

"You'll live to be well over a hundred and one" was always their father's reply.

The boys often asked if dad had a girlfriend or several girlfriends, as mummy had had a few boyfriends in the years following their divorce. Sometimes they worried that he might be lonely, because the boys always had one another, so they never felt lonely. However, if one was ever poorly, the other would look over and sit, or lie, besides them until they returned to full health. It was usually Ben who was poorly with ear and throat infections. Will seemed robust to everything the world had to offer, even when gastroenteritis affected many of the children in their classroom one spring. If he ever fell off his bicycle or from the tree, he would usually be dosed up with arnica or another 'one of Grandma's magic potions.' Then he would be made to rest for a little while. Will was far more daring than Ben and often more outspoken too. Ben would often watch in horror, as Will would climb branches far higher than even Daddy would attempt.

Grandma used to say that she would ask the fairies and the angels to watch over them both - always. Sometimes she would appear, just as Will was about to do his 'Dare Devil' finale. She'd tempt him from the tree with freshly made lemonade or orangeade, or just say that she was collecting them because she would be taking them for a walk or out shopping. How was it that she always just seemed to know? The times the youngsters had sat in the garden, the trees, or the den, discussing how she knew the precise timing they would surely never know?

Going shopping with Grandma was always such fun. She knew most of the stall holders on the local market and they would often be given samples of various breads, cheeses, cakes and pastries. If they went before mealtimes, it was hard to eat when they got back to the house and yet she never scolded them. Mum on the other hand was boring and would usually order food on line as she said they were always *so naughty in the supermarkets.* Either Grandma, or Daddy would take them shopping for shoes, trainers and clothes, including their school uniforms, which they found the most boring of all. They were usually told that afterwards they could have a treat in the toy store, or they would be taken down to the local beach to play, swim or do skimming on the water with the flat stones.

They often wondered what it would be like to have Grandpa around. Sometimes they would catch Grandma looking sad, or perhaps with tears in her eyes when she looked at his favourite photograph. When they asked her if she missed Grandpa, she would always be honest and say 'she missed him and his laughter, his eyes and his smiles, his cuddles and his kisses.' Then she would run after them and chase them both around the house, tickling them and making them laugh.

Oh what fun she was! They often asked her age and she would reply 'as old as my tongue and a little bit older than my teeth.' Sometimes they would ask if she were a hundred. They'd laugh when she rolled her eyes and told them off for being so cheeky. She never smacked them and rarely raised her voice. However, if she ever caught them climbing too high, whether it was the climbing frames, or in the trees, she would get very cross indeed. Neither boy could believe just how loud her voice would be, as she shouted them down and made them sit on the door steps for time-out.

They knew when they had upset her as she would always be quiet afterwards. They truly hated that, so learnt not to upset her too often. They were of course rare occasions anyways, though as Will grew older, his feistiness was becoming more and more noticeable.

PART TWO

Chapter Ten

Sheila was very aware of Will's feistiness especially as she had her own son after all and also two other grandsons. She had grown up with four older brothers whom she dearly loved and had herself been a bit of a 'Tomboy' in her earlier years.

Her thoughts drifted back in time to distant memories. Little did her grandsons know how much trouble she used to get into growing up around the London dock yard. That was until her best friend Michael fell from the rigging of an old, disused cruise liner one summer. On that fateful day she truly thought that her heart would surely break.

She had cried for several days and refused to eat too. She would often remember the sound as his body hit the wooden deck. It had been so long ago and yet still she could recall that fatal fall and the depth of the emptiness that followed. They had both climbed that rigging over a thousand times, both of them were daring enough to look down and pretend to be pirates looking out to sea. That fateful day, a sudden wind had caught him off guard and made him loosen his grip on the rigging, together with the combination of what seemed the loudest sound of a ship's siren and the seagulls screeches, he lost his grip completely. Watching his body fall seemed to take forever. It was as if time stood completely still. Listening to the thud as he landed was even worse. No moans, nor groans, no screams, nor shouts, oh how she ached to hear for that one sound. Any sound would do. Anything, but the deadly silence.

It was dawn before they were found. His limp body had remained where it had landed and although the seagulls pecked at his face frequently, she was too frozen with fear to move. The shouts of the police search team, the local volunteers and seafarers fell on deaf ears. As they lifted her into their arms and wrapped her in a blanket, they offered her food and a warm drink. She asked them to make sure he was alright as he hadn't spoken to her since he fell. She was in a state of total shock and did not speak any other words for several months. As she was handed over to her parents, Mr and Mrs Brown, Clara, her mother cried tears of relief and her father cuddled her tightly, rather than scolding her as he usually did.

On the journey home she thought of her best friend. She remembered watching a lighter, less solid, 'see through' version of him raise above his body moments after the fall and go up into the sky. He had looked down on her and smiled. She knew that this must mean that his soul was making its way to heaven. She had, at that moment at least, felt an intense peace come over her. Recalling his face now, she wondered what it must be like to be in heaven.

Arriving home she was put straight to bed. The police said they would send a female officer in the morning to question the young lady. They explained that there were no suspicious circumstances and nothing to be concerned about. Sheila didn't understand what 'suspicious circumstances' meant though when she tried to ask, even her mouth would not move, nor even make a sound.

She hardly slept. In the morning she was awakened when her parents explained that she would be interviewed by 'the nice police lady.' Poor Sheila was to be mute for quite some time. She kept weeping and shaking randomly throughout the day. Her mother was busy with her brothers and the household chores, not to mention washing other people's laundry as a supplement for her husband's poor wage. Throughout those long days, Sheila would sleep often and when she was awake would think of Michael's face smiling back at her. Whenever she felt able, she would help with the dishes or the washing.

Her mother used to sing and hum to the children, though now all she seemed to do was shout and sigh often. They were deep long sighs and she would hold her hands on her hips trying to catch her breath. She was a stout woman with deep wrinkles and a huge chest, which Sheila loved to snuggle into when they had a rare, quiet moment.

Michael's mother Fanny, had often called around previously for a cuppa and a natter, as she too washed others laundry to make ends meet. The two women would laugh, howl and often dance and sing together in the kitchen, whilst the water heated on the open fire. Both had hands raw and often bleeding, by the time they had finished the day's work.

Fanny never came near the house ever again after the loss of her son. Sheila felt the sadness as her mother missed her best friend. They had grown up together and when Fanny was widowed some two years earlier, they had shared so much closeness and *so many tears*. Now Sheila watched on in her own private world of grief and intense sadness. If she could speak and tell them what she had seen that fateful day would they believe her? Would they believe that she saw a ghost like version of him rise towards the sky?

Her mouth would open for a drink, though only occasionally for food and often she would just throw it back up. Her mother made her eat outside now, as she was exhausted cleaning up the vomit and the smell was abhorrent too. There was a silence between them, as Sheila watched her mother now and her mother's eyes held such pain.

Since becoming mute, Sheila wondered if she could or would, ever speak again. Throughout this time, her hearing had become ever sharper.

"It's the funeral tomorrow and the lads at the factory have said that we are *not invited*. If we go, or even stand near the graveyard, then the Bradleys will beat us all to within an inch of our lives." Though barely more than a whisper, she clearly heard her father explain that they were not welcome at the funeral. He was clearly very saddened and shaken up. A man of very few words and even less emotions, the impact this had upon them both, especially him; at having to relay the news to his wife, was devastating.

Sheila's mother had hoped for reconciliation. The message was absolutely crystal clear and this *would definitely not* be the case.

Chapter Eleven

Several months later the family moved to the countryside, as her father had been offered a position on a farm. It was owned by a huge landowner. One of his cousins had worked here for many years. Things had never been the same since that fateful evening. Sheila's brothers were excited at the prospect to be living closely with relatives whom they usually only saw at Christmas, or on other special occasions, like weddings and funerals. The word 'funeral' was banned in their household and father would take his belt to anyone of them that '*dared mention that word.*' Sheila had heard her mother crying throughout the day of Michael's funeral. She thought Sheila hadn't heard her sobbing, though by now her hearing was like that of an owl. The acuteness of her own hearing astounded her.

Sheila's intuition and creativity had also expanded rapidly around this time too and her artwork was much more detailed. It seemed to be alive at times. She would take pen and paper, or usually pencil to sketch anything at all, just to pass the time of day. Being silent often meant that she was living in her own world and, as she had lost the confidence to leave the house, she turned towards her artwork for solace.

She was looking forwards to moving to the country as she would be able to draw the wildlife, the gardens, beautiful cottages and manor houses. The architecture here was inspiring to her and she loved the tall red brick chimneys and the buildings where they stored the hops and grains. It was so different from London town and much quieter too. On their previous visits she had loved the gardens, the colours, the huge variety of plants, flowers, bushes, shrubs and trees. She had always felt at complete peace and oneness here.

The thoughts of moving here lifted her spirits and she knew intuitively that the whole family would benefit. Her mother had really taken the loss of her friend Fanny so badly, not to mention little Michael. She had loved having him around her feet and sneaking off with her scones and cakes she had baked; even when he yelped as they burnt his fingertips! She missed his mischievous grin and the general mischief too, despite having felt that most of the time she had shouted at him constantly.

"My, if only I could turn the clock back time and give him one last cuddle, instead of a clout around his earhole, or his arse!" she had said without even thinking on the morning of the funeral. Little did Clara know that Sheila had heard her words so very clearly uttered. She had wept for well over an hour, as those precious memories of her beloved best friend broke her heart.

Despite all the upset and hostility towards them, the dirty looks, or sometimes just the ignorance of the local folks, her parent's marriage had remained strong. Yet the lines upon her mother's face and brow had deepened. The whole family was so relieved at the thought of moving on to fresh pastures.

Mum was a really great cook and baked amazing cakes, breads and scones too. There was a position of cook's assistant in the huge manor house. As the family were growing up now and they would have support of other family members around, it seemed quite pertinent to take the job. Her husband had suggested that it might just help take her mind off things and if nothing else, would ease her into the community and get her to make new friends.

So, one Saturday morning the family packed everything up and set off on a steam train to Kent. They had been renting a house near the docks which was furnished and they had been promised a furnished cottage by the edge of the field in Kent, also known as the Garden Of England. To her mother, the thought of open space and the delight of open fields, rather than back to back terraced houses was quite appealing. Knowing the children could play openly and would grow up away from busy roads and *so much smoke* was delightful.

She had worried about Sheila since that fateful evening. Her last words had been asking about Michael's well-being when the police had arrived. Since then, the silence had been deafening to both of them. Her brothers seemed okay, though she was aware that they did act much more cautiously around their 'baby sister.'

Arriving at the nearest station, they were thrilled to see Cousin Bill ready to collect them with the horse and cart. Their belongings were placed on the cart and then they too were perched on the rickety old thing. Listening to the whistle and the now familiar sounds of the train leaving the station, they knew for certain that they had made the right decision. This place held a magical peace and a deep serenity. It was perfect for a family of seven, who had been through so much in the last few months.

As they approached the huge gates leading onto the estate, they turned left towards the manor house. It was so impressive in all its majesty, as it sat at the top of a hillock surrounded and graced by immaculate lawns and gardens. To the right, they followed a track which seemed to get narrower and narrower, as they turned the corner, there was a row of cottages by the side of the field with the river in the distance too. The sound of nothing-ness was refreshing.

Apart from the birds and the wildlife, there was very little else. As Sheila's mother looked around at her children, she felt a peace descend upon her. Sheila herself sat with her favourite brother Harry. They were snuggled together on the cart as they neared their new home. Since the accident, he had made much more time for his baby sister and he was obviously reassuring her that all would be well. Despite the fact they all knew she could see clearly, he was pointing out the trees and the out-buildings, as if she had also lost her sight too. Her mother looked on, grateful of the love her children shared.

"Almost there now" Cousin Bob shouted.

"Yours is the end cottage, the one with the arched door."

Her husband's hand reached for hers and he gave her that look that she had known for so long now; saying, without the need for words, that they had definitely made the right decision. As the worry lines on his brow began to disappear, she glanced over at him as he watched each of their children's faces when the cart slowed to a halt. The excitement was clear. They were obviously delighted to start a new life, with new adventures and new playmates.

Within a few minutes they were unpacked. The windows were opened to allow the fresh air into the bones of this old cottage. It seemed to breathe in a sigh of relief, as it had clearly been empty for quite some time. Bob's wife had left some groceries on the table, fresh bread, cheeses, fruit and vegetables, not to mention one of her prized cakes and some scones too. Warm soup in a huge pan bubbled on the Aga. What a treat. What a welcome this was indeed. Bob said he would call back in a few hours. He and his wife only lived three doors down in the terrace of cottages anyways.

They soon tucked into a hearty lunch and as their father allocated the bedrooms. They all knew they were meant to be here, without a single shadow of a doubt. Within an hour of their arrival, with feather duster in hand and a bucket of hot water Sheila's mother had the place looking homely.

Once they had been allocated bedrooms, Sheila and her brother Harry wandered around the whole house. Then Harry asked if she wanted to venture outside. They were reasonably familiar with the area, as they had come for short stays over the years. Being here, a place they had loved for so long, knowing that this was now to be their home, was really wonderful and uplifting.

They knew of a local wood and Harry explained to their mother that were they were off to explore. Since the accident, Sheila had rarely left her mother's side and was never allowed out alone. Harry was a bright, intelligent young man with a huge amount of common-sense. He was probably the most compassionate of all the boys.

Her mother breathed a huge sigh of relief that her daughter was now safe from the threats that the Bradleys had in mind back in London. Once they had closed the door behind them, without realising, instant tears of relief welled in her eyes. She gasped as her husband wrapped his arms around her waist and pulled her close, slapping a huge kiss upon her lips. When he saw her tears, he dried them away with his handkerchief and smiled a knowing smile at her. Taking both of her hands in his, he made his opinion very clear;

"My dearest wife and love of my life. I might be a man of few emotions and few words. You've known me long enough now to know that when I say something, I mean what I say. So, I tell you *now that I know IN MY SOUL* we are all to be happy here, putting all the other stuff behind us. We have a bright new future ahead and despite the fact that we will both have to work hard, in order to earn the respect of the locals and the land owner, I know that our children will grow up here to be happy and contented. They will have a better life than we could offer them in the city and hopefully our Sheila will be herself again soon".

With that speech out of the way, he pulled out a package from under his waistcoat. When he opened it, he showed her the pencils and paintbrushes too.

"I asked Cousin Bob to get her an easel too, so she can paint, draw, or sketch whatever, and whenever, she wants to. This I think, is a great way to encourage her to settle into her new life. Our Bob had mentioned to the land owner Mr Marsh of that awful evening's events. He has requested we meet later this evening at the manor house. He wants to see us both at 8pm."

The dusk soon came and by now, everyone had settled into their new home. As instructed, Sheila's parents walked up to the manor house at 7.30pm, knowing they would arrive in good time. They were greeted by Mr Marsh and his wife Mildred too. They had never been into the manor house before and were so impressed by the huge ceilings, massive life-like portraits and the beautifully finished furniture and furnishings.

Once they were shown into the lounge, Mr Marsh expressed their sadness, when they had heard of the reason why they had decided to come to live here. He expressed his delight to be able to welcome them here personally. He continued to explain that both he and his wife hoped they liked the cottage and that it was to their satisfaction. The conversation then moved on, as he said that he had purchased several acres of land locally, which they would be farming and that the cook was looking forward to 'another pair of hands' in the kitchen.

As they were served tea and scones, it was clear that this man had a huge presence together with a kind and sincere heart. He made small talk about their journey and the asked about the rest of their family. He explained that his children had left long ago and were in various places across the U.K. One was in America too. The love between him and his wife was clearly obvious. She merely sat and nodded, acknowledging and being acknowledged, as and when requested. She was a tiny woman with eyes which seemed far too small for her to be able to see anything. Sheila's mother wasn't too sure what to make of her, though her mind was made up that she already liked Mr Marsh.

Once they were refreshed Mr Marsh asked if they would please follow him. He led them through to the left wing of the house. Opening a huge panelled door which had obviously not been opened for quite some time, he showed them a room which was set out with many easels and canvases. They were all of differing sizes and shapes, some half-finished, some very nearly finished and some completely blank. As Sheila's mother's eyes scanned the room, there were so many different quills, inkpots, chalks and oil paints, that she found herself suppressing what would have been a huge gasp. Covering her excitement with a slight cough and passing a knowing look across to her husband, she smiled a huge smile of relief. Sometimes in life, against all odds, the right jigsaw pieces do indeed fit together perfectly.

"I believe that you have an artist in your family and I believe that art work can be very useful in the healing process. You know your daughter best, though I would like you to bring her here, as soon as you feel that she would like to come and take a look. Your sons are also welcome here too. I am happy to arrange for her to receive private tuition here also. I was told that she had not been well enough to attend school since that unfortunate evening. Of course I will incur all the costs as you have your family to raise. Rest assured, I will do my best and I hope that she will be able to put this incident and the sad loss of her dear friend behind her." Mr Marsh clearly stated his best intentions for Sheila.

Sheila's parents were thrilled and delighted. They nodded and shook hands with him, showing their deepest and most heartfelt appreciation.

"My brother Joseph was injured in the war and came to stay with us whilst he recovered. His artwork kept him sane, as he dealt with losing his left leg and all the atrocities he had witnessed. I trust this is satisfactory to you?"

Never did it cross their mind that the owner of the docklands in London was also called Mr Marsh. The brothers had so many different businesses. The two men got together often in London to discuss their father's investments and how best to use the monies. Both funded orphanages and church schools locally. They had often discussed the plight of that poor family on that wretched evening, when the young boy had fallen from the ships rigging.

Mr Marsh had been warned well over a year ago that children were playing in the yard. He was also warned that the particular cruiser on which the accident occurred, should by now, have been dismantled for scrap metal. He had been advised also to form a secure perimeter around the docklands, as the locals had expressed concerns that children could possibly drown. Having too much to do and too little time, meant that it had simply got overlooked more times than Mr Marsh could care to recall. Once again guilt for their actions became a huge motive in their philanthropy.

Both brothers had always suspected that their father had gained his fortune by 'ill-gotten means' and both were keen to keep that from the public eye. They were both present by his side when he had died. They had listened intently to his final prayers of repentance, as he made his way to rest with 'The Lord.' He had asked for forgiveness for all he had done, telling them the truth as to how his vast fortune had been obtained, through slavery, theft, prostitution and other 'inappropriate means.'

As they listened to him breathe out his last breath, they vowed to make amends as per his wishes and in doing so, hoped they would keep a tight lid on the family secret.

Chapter Twelve

The next few days were simple though busy. Sheila's older brothers were also requested to work the land, though they could attend school as, and when, they wanted. Both boys were intelligent and could read and write. They were looking forwards to having money in their pockets and getting stuck in, working the land and feeling their way through the ropes. They wondered what it would be like to be like real working men. As there were two of them, they had each other for company too. Each morning they would set out with their father and work until dusk. They were welcome to visit the manor house at any time for food and refreshments, although mostly these things were brought out to them. They settled in very well indeed and soon managed to entice the local girls by their London accent too!

The two younger boys were settled in the local school. They enjoyed themselves and both thrived very quickly. At the weekends, if needed, they would help on the farm. They were happy to learn how to milk the cows, help the blacksmith to shoe the horses and how to clean out the stables. Harry was also keen to learn carpentry. He had lovingly carved many items from wood over the years.

The youngest son Charlie was keen to *just be*. He loved to watch the gardener and would often be found in the potting sheds, planting seeds and taking cuttings. Mr and Mrs Marsh enjoyed looking over the gardens, especially the fountains and the lake with the fish. Seeing how little Charlie was captivated by nature and how much he loved the garden, they would often slip a few pennies to Mr Thomas, the head gardener to pass to Charlie, for all his hard work.

He had a secret jar in his den, which no one knew existed. He decided he would let that money grow, as if he had planted a money tree, until in his own mind at least, he was old enough to be a gentleman.

Clara was thrilled that her precious family all settled so quickly and so well. To be honest there was no reason for them not to do so. She had always encouraged them to listen to their hearts and their intuition, to stick together and look out for one another. *'United we stand and divided we fall'* was her motto and they understood. Since that fateful evening they had all become closer, through experiencing the shock and the threats, even from other school children. Here they were, not by chance it seemed, as everything slipped into place so easily. It was as if it were predestined.

Sheila's father loved it here and the man of little emotions ebbed away to create a man of great humour and even more affection, than she had ever imagined possible. Something in him had softened and for that she was incredibly grateful indeed. At the end of the day he would ask all their sons about their days. If ever any of them seemed upset, or distracted, he would always get to the bottom of it and restore harmony once more.

She herself loved her new life. She had always got along with her husband's family and was welcomed into the manor house. She was encouraged to settle in and enjoy herself with all the other staff too. She and the cook could often be heard laughing and giggling, singing and were even known to dance in the kitchens; even on the hottest and most humid of summer's days. All in all, life was good and she was the definitely the happiest she had ever been.

Within just over a fortnight of arriving here, Sheila started talking again and could be heard singing to the birds and the other wildlife. All the family sighed a huge sigh of relief and none ever spoke of Michael, unless she did. Occasionally, usually completely out of the blue, she would mention him and what they used to do together and the pranks they had pulled. More often than not, she would smile and say how much she missed him and wished he was here to witness and indeed, be a part of their new life.

True to his word, Mr Marsh paid for her private tuition up at the house and she was supported in all aspects of her artwork too. She often took the carved birds that Harry had created with her to sketch or paint. She loved using sepia and charcoal too. Both Mr and Mrs Marsh would often sit with her and the encouragement she received from them was truly touching. If he was ever away on business; which was quite often, he would always make a point to visit her and her family in the cottage upon his return.

One particular morning, several months after their arrival in Kent, as she walked up the driveway to the house she met Mr Marsh who had been out for his usual morning stroll. She was laden with a heavy basket and he enquired just what was so heavy, as she looked like she would keel over at any moment from the weight. As he offered to carry the basket, she explained that they were a collection of carvings her brother had made of both wood and stone. When they set the basket down upon the small side table, she unpacked the carvings with deepest respect and reverence for her brother's artwork. Clearly impressed at the precision and quality of workmanship that was unfolding here, he was inspired to summon her parents that very evening requesting them to attend dinner with him and his wife. He asked Sheila if it was satisfactory that she leave the items here and he would promise their safekeeping.

Her parents were obviously nervous that night as they both wore their best clothes. As she tied up her hair into a braid, Sheila placed the wildflowers she had collected earlier that day, in her mother's greying hair. Delighted with the result of her work, her parents set out on their journey to the manor house. They were greeted at the door by the butler, who was by now a dear friend to them, before being shown into the drawing room. Mr and Mrs Marsh soon appeared and they were offered drinks and canapes.

As the evening went on, Mr Marsh requested the private company of her husband. They retired into the drawing room, whilst Sheila's mother was escorted to the left wing by Mrs Marsh to view her daughter's very impressive work. Her mother was amazed at the beautiful sketches and paintings. She gasped when she was shown samples of Sheila's handwriting too. Mrs Marsh was clearly thrilled that Sheila's mother was delighted with her progress and promised that they would do their very best to bring Sheila's talents out. Their commitment to her daughter was most touching and she expressed her gratitude for all they had done.

"She's a treasure and a delight to have around the house and for the first time in years, I myself have felt inspired to paint and to write poetry." Mrs Marsh was clearly enjoying having the company of Sheila in their home.

Meanwhile, in the drawing room both men drank brandy and as Mr Marsh showed Sheila's father the carvings and stonemasonry work that his son had produced. He too was clearly impressed.

“How old is your son?” asked Mr Marsh.

“He has a wonderful gift and as soon as he is 15, I would like to add his name to a project of mine abroad. He will be given instruction on restoring an old cathedral and then maintaining it too. To be honest, I know the boy has talent, I’ve seen enough projects through over the years, and I really believe that this young man could learn to manage the whole project. Over time, perhaps he could oversee the other projects that I am dealing with across the world. Your family has the quality of integrity Mr Browne, and that is something which cannot be overestimated, nor can it be learnt. Trust means much to a man of my status. Both trust and respect are necessary in all aspects of my work. I earn the men’s trust and they earn mine. Without trust we are nothing.”

Mr Marsh turned to face the window as he thought of his father’s indiscretions. He had to pause for a few moments and clear his throat before he continued.

“I know Sheila and Harry are most close, please appreciate that I would never cause any upset to this young lady, especially now as she is settling so well into her new life. Your son will be well cared for whilst he is away. I promise that he will return every few months, for a fortnight’s break to be with his family for the first two years whilst he learns the ropes. Then we shall see what he wants to do.”

“I watch your children and they all have a great work ethic. A rare quality if I might say so. Little Charlie is loved by the gardener and the blacksmith too. With your consent, I am happy to find him work once his schooling days are over. Your two elder boys are thriving and growing up to be quite handsome young men. Their employment with me will also continue."

Clara's husband was amazed at this man's thoughtfulness and his directness. He had known about Charlie's love of gardening and yet hadn't known of the extent of Harry's abilities. When he was shown the carvings, he was so proud. His son had often brought home bits and bobs that he had created, yet here clearly was so much talent. Here also was a way of securing his future.

"Please do not feel you need to make a decision this evening on any part of this conversation. I look forward to your answer within the fortnight though, if that is satisfactory to you and your good wife."

Later that evening, whilst snuggling up to one another after all these years, Mr Browne announced that;

"We have a marvellous brood of children my dear Clara" and he expressed his heartfelt pride. The peace and love between them was complete and they slept wrapped up in each other's arms.

Chapter Thirteen

Harrys leaving was both heart breaking and a wonderful celebration all rolled into one. His father gave him a smile and a man hug whilst telling him just how proud he was to have a son as talented. He advised him that he should make the most of this opportunity. He told him that he would always have a place to live if things didn't work out. They would say a prayer for him before each evening meal. He also gave him a single gold coin, which he had found whilst working the field one day. He had checked with Mr Marsh whether he was alright to keep it and his employer has certainly happy that he should indeed.

The two big brothers punched him playfully in the chest. Clara was filled with so much pride she thought she would burst open from the chest. A thousand tears seemed to flow from her eyes at his leaving. She had packed lots of his favourite foods; cakes, biscuits and scones. Charlie, choking back the tears and struggling to get his words out, said he would miss his big brother and would mark each and every day on the tree trunk, near their secret den, until he returned.

Sheila was doing her best to hold back the tears. Though she had known this day would come for many months, when it finally arrived it was heart-wrenching. If losing Michael was hard, then this would be even tougher. Even though she now had support from so many sources and was certainly growing up into a beautiful young woman, she knew she would miss her favourite brother desperately.

Of course she wanted the best for him, knowing that he would certainly rise to the occasion and blossom in the field of restoration.

He certainly had an incredible gift indeed. All of the siblings had always been encouraged to be true to their hearts and follow what was right for them. Letters were promised and upon Mr Marsh's return in a few weeks, he would bring news of how her brother was settling in and enjoying the new experiences.

Sheila passed him a card which she had handmade for her favourite brother. He had refused to leave her side from that fateful evening well over a year ago, until she returned to full health. As they hugged one another, both knew the power of their connection. Just as she had often felt Michael around, since he passed over, so she also knew that she would also feel a huge connection to her big brother. Tears flowed from their eyes as they separated and everything was packed into the cart. He was travelling with Mr Marsh in the carriage. Later they would catch the train and then fly to the locality. As they all waved him off, they stood together, each with their own private thoughts and memories. Each sibling knew that this would be the start of them all growing up and going out into the big wide world.

Clara had organised a celebration meal for her boy, which now eaten, meant that everything needed to be cleared away. She was glad of the distraction in the kitchen, whilst the boys went to the den. Sheila and her father helped tidy around in the kitchen and lounge.

The three of them then sat in the garden which Charlie had tamed after so many years of neglect. His knew his mother loved roses. The gardener appreciated his help so much in the stately home gardens. They would often spend their spare time here at the cottage, sorting through the weeds, thistles and brambles. They loved restoring it back to its former glory or 'non-existent former glory,' as they would call it and then laugh together. The fences were fixed up too with Harrys help and assistance. He had even made a sun-dial and a bird bath.

As they sat on the garden bench that Harry had carved from an old tree trunk, Sheila went back into the house, saying that she had forgotten something. When she returned, she carried a heavy package wrapped in a chequered cloth and brown paper. Placing it on the table, she looked up at her parents and asked them to unwrap it together. Looking at one another in confusion, they rose to the table to open the mystery parcel. Once unravelled and unwrapped, they found four hand carved roses set into a heart shaped bowl. Harry had obviously managed to keep it a secret from them and the intricacy of his work was so touching that once again, Mrs Browne burst into tears. There was a note attached from Harry which read:

'Dear Ma and Pa, this is to remind you of how much I truly love you. Dearest Mum, I know the rose is your favourite flower and that you have always told us to let our hearts be open, just like the petals of the rose, to allow the sweetness of life into our hearts and then in turn to feed our soul. This wisdom I will carry with me on my journey. I wanted you to know that wherever I am, you have both given me a huge foundation stone with good morals and manners.

Dearest Father, I have watched you over the years work hard to feed and clothe us all. I know things have been so much easier since we moved here and I know, as I have started to grow into a young man, that I now begin to appreciate why you instilled such discipline, commitment and determination into us. *'Never give up when you feel that what you are doing is right,'* is a motto I shall hold close to my heart.

Look after our family and keep smiling. Mind you, quit with the rubbish jokes! I'll miss you all and think of you each and every day.'

Touching words indeed from an ever grateful son.

Chapter Fourteen

Sheila missed Harry daily and thought of him often. She wondered what he would be doing and who he would meet, who would inspire him and take care of him. She thought of all the people he would have the opportunity to inspire too. She had watched Mr Marsh and despite her youth, she was wise enough to know, that he would do his utmost to provide her brother with the right opportunities for his growth and fulfilment.

Since his leaving, she had found her artwork had changed. It had become more colourful and slightly abstract at times too. Mrs Marsh checked in with her daily. Sheila thought it was because she was missing her husband, although she never said so. Life at home had gone on in pretty much the same way these last few weeks. Both her eldest brothers were spending more and more time at the local public house and also with the girls. Her father would often remind them 'not to get their fingers burnt.' What on earth he meant, when they were seeing girls, she had no idea, though her brother's both laughed and mother usually blushed, then coughed, whenever it was mentioned.

Charlie obviously missed his elder brother and despite getting more and more involved in gardening, often she would catch him seeming to be in a world of his own. Sometimes he certainly did shed some tears too, though only in her presence 'so as not to upset ma' he would say. Harry had certainly left a gap in all their lives. They knew that they just had to do their best to make the most of what they had. Trusting too, that all was working out for him. Father often called Charlie, 'Harry' by mistake and would then apologise to him, though Charlie always said he was pleased that his brother was not forgotten.

Her thoughts often drifted to Michael and sometimes she thought that she heard his voice whisper to her. Often it was in connection with her artwork, usually when she was thoroughly engaged in wildlife painting or sketching. Sometimes it was when she was sewing too. Mrs Marsh was a keen and talented embroiderer and was encouraging Sheila to make small items at first to gain her confidence. Sheila enjoyed embroidering tiny flowers into handkerchiefs and napkins. Mrs Marsh was a quiet soul and though there were many silences between them, especially whilst they concentrated, never was there any uncomfortableness.

Soon Mr Marsh would return. She was looking forward to listening to the stories of how Harry was progressing and how he had settled in.

Chapter Fifteen

The news of Harry's progress was very positive and everyone was delighted that he had settled in and was enjoying the work too. Mr Marsh said that he was even learning the language and although wary of trying new foods at first, now he was certainly bulking out. He was also becoming a respected member of the team of specialists in the art of restoration. The work was on target and they were assured that he would return home within three months.

Those three months whizzed by for all of them and one bright sunny morning a horse and cart could be heard in the distance. Sheila was the first to hear it and knowing it would be her favourite brother, she was up and dressed in a flash. She managed to wake up the rest of the household quite easily. As she opened the door, keen to get to her brother before her mother smothered him in kisses and tears, there he was larger than life. Now he was almost six feet tall and seemed to have even bigger shoulders and muscles. He lifted her up in his arms with hardly any effort at all and was then welcomed into the home by the rest of the family.

As usual mother had prepared some food the night before and as they all tucked in, they were keen to listen to Harry's adventures and travels. The driver of the horse and cart had ventured up to the manor house, as instructed by Mr Marsh and was to rest easy after the journey.

Harry was obviously thrilled to be home, though they were all surprised that he didn't seem tired at all. His voice deeper than ever, he passed around some architects sketches to show what they had been working on. He was excited and was so obviously thoroughly loving his new life. It was also clear that he had missed them too and their broad accents. Most of the men were locals in the French community. He had had to learn the language quickly and since few of them had ever travelled to England, or knew the language. The French accent and language sounded incredibly different to the English, which was all they had ever known.

Harry's sense of humour was still very evident, as he relayed some of the pranks and practical jokes he had pulled on his workmates. He would ask them to get him a glass hammer and a long stand for example. They were never quite able to match his antics, though he knew they were becoming quick learners. His mannerisms and everything about him radiated a sense of love, respect, dedication and grace for his work, the culture and the people. He explained that on his rest day every week he would travel to the coast to catch some fish with the other workmen. Friendships were forming and connections being made easily. The locals nicknamed him 'The Englishman with a great talent,' which had their father and the two eldest brothers in stitches of laughter, whilst mother just blushed. The local cuisine was becoming normal to him now and he enjoyed eating and drinking with the locals. He said he could manage simple conversations and was looking forward to being able to converse more easily within the coming months.

His skin was tanned. His hands hard and toughened from his work. Conversation continued as he did his best to explain the different types of French cheeses which were called fromage.

"From where" Mr Browne would reply, whenever he mentioned that word, or forgot to use English version. Needless to say they would all burst into laughter frequently.

They finished the meal and it was suggested that they all allow him time to rest after his long journey. It was lovely to have him home again, though they knew that the time was precious and his return date would soon arrive. His snoring could be heard echoing through the cottage within minutes, so they all headed into the garden. There was no usual weekend routine here in Kent. The weather determined many things, as often they would have to harvest the field's, whilst the weather was kindly. The local community was just that, one huge community. Often they would be invited to someone's house for a meal or a sing-song. The two older boys would often go fishing or swimming in the local river if they got the opportunity, which in all fairness was quite rare. Sometimes they would simply sleep off a hangover from the previous evening's card games.

Charlie and Sheila were always happy gardening together. He would tend to the garden and she would sketch whatever took her fancy. Today seemed strange as they were *all together* for once, which was a rare.

"I'll pop the kettle on" Clara said as she sensed the unusualness of them all being here together. By the time she returned, they were all laughing and joking, chatting easily with one another and ready to start eating whatever their mother could rustle up.

"You've only just eaten you greedy buggers" she howled laughing, as she looked on proudly at their three sons.

"Come on Sheila lets bake some scones and leave the menfolk to men talk."

Sheila loved cooking and it was so lovely to spend time with everyone together again. She hoped Harry would soon be up, though from the sound of the snoring it seemed most unlikely!

Chapter Sixteen

Sheila loved the life which she now led. Harry's visits inevitably became fewer and fewer. Over the next four years as she approached adulthood, her artwork became even more detailed. Her paintings were so beautiful that often people would wonder and would ponder whether or not it was a painting or a photograph. She remained determined to learn and improve her work consistently.

One spring afternoon, the manor house bell rang and Sheila could hear surprised gasps from Mr and Mrs Marsh. She looked across at her tutor who suggested they continue with their studies. Within an hour, both she and her teacher Miss Black were invited for tea in the drawing room. They were told that Mr and Mrs Marsh had visitors from London and that they would love to meet Sheila and her teacher. Introductions were made and they all enjoyed the light luncheon.

Mr Marsh explained that he and Mr King had met in college many years earlier. After leaving, they had established a construction and restoration business. He knew Harry well and they had become well acquainted. He explained what a wonderful craftsman he was and how patient and respected as a teacher with the new apprentices he had become. It was clear that they all respected Harry. Sheila smiled as she thought of her dearest brother.

"I believe that you too are most artistic and creative. Mr and Mrs Marsh have just been explaining to us about how you came here and how you have thrived. If it's agreeable to you, we would love to look at your artwork please?

Sheila nodded her approval and said:

"Yes that would be fine, I am happy to show you some of my favourite drawing and sketches, although some are at home in the cottage." Mr Marsh suggested that after lunch they go through to the study and have a look together.

Their delight when they saw the incredible detail in her work was most evident. They were interested in her wildlife paintings, both the simple sketches and the finished articles, architectural paintings and charcoal drawings. They were also most impressed by her ability to be so diverse with the use of a variety of different art mediums.

"You definitely have a great talent young lady. We will let you continue with your studies. Thank you for sharing these beautiful pieces with us. Well done." As they left the room, Sheila blushed crimson with pride.

Several days later Mr Marsh called in the cottage to see Sheila's parents. He thought that Sheila might be there too and he was happy for her to be included in the conversation. He explained that the Kings had visited and been highly impressed with Sheila's work. He and Mr King had a rapidly expanding construction and restoration business. They were desperate to employ talented architects. Seeing her work and knowing that Sheila was most capable at mathematics too would be a perfect combination for her to be enrolled as an ideal student.

Sheila had known that since the Kings had visited, Mr Marsh had something planned as he visited her daily, rather than his usual twice a week whilst she was studying. He had also carefully selected her artwork which included the manor house, the village hall and all the local churches. He had asked if he could borrow them for a few days. She had of course agreed, knowing that he would take great care of them.

"The Kings feel it would be of value to you if we all visit the architectural college later this week. I am happy to make the arrangements if this is agreeable to you all. If you like the place, you are welcome to start as soon as you are ready Sheila."

They all looked around at one another knowing that now was the time for Sheila too to leave the nest. They all passed on their agreement to Mr Marsh. Arrangements were made for the Friday of that week.

When they arrived, they were shown around the grounds and then into a huge hallway. Drawings of cathedrals and churches, stately homes and great architectural works of art lined the walls. They were taken through to a huge study were Mr King was waiting to receive his guests. Sheila could feel her father's pride and her mother's sadness that another of her children was about to leave the nest. Sheila herself felt that she had already known this place. She was comfortable and knew that she would settle easily, despite being one of very few female students.

After refreshments and welcomes, they were shown around the various classrooms, gymnasium, swimming baths and the grand hall too. The place was astounding. It was filled with breath-taking architecture and Sheila's eyes really weren't quite sure just what to focus on. She knew she belonged here without question. She had made her decision.

Chapter Seventeen

Sheila studied with masses of determination and although she struggled with certain aspects of the work, she always found that the teachers were patient in their explanations to her. She was well-liked and settled very quickly. She was soon encouraged to express her opinions on new buildings and also restoration projects too. In the main her ideas were welcomed and appreciated.

The day she met William she almost passed out. They were invited to the opening of a cathedral which had recently been restored. As they stood looking up at the sacred geometry in the ceiling, their eyes met once they were returning their necks to their normal state. He smiled at her and as soon as they had finished the tour, he motioned towards her and made his intentions very clear. Sheila's sharp intuition informed her that indeed this was to be the man she would in fact spend the rest of her life with.

They were married within three months and Mr Marsh offered them a cottage of their own in the grounds of the college. They were incredibly happy and both highly respected, capable students. He specialised in the new and she in the old. They really were quite a combination. The love that they had for one another shone through and they brought so much love to other students and those they worked with.

Whilst in their years of study, they had met a Mediterranean man called Alexander who they soon named 'Alexander The Great.' He was clearly very capable, yet his English skills sadly lacking. They welcomed him into their home often. They delighted in learning from him about the many architectural wonders from across the world that he had visited with his family since his early childhood.

He shared the wisdom of the Greek culture and the stories of the Gods and Goddesses. His father had a massive architectural business and he had travelled extensively across most of the globe. Their friendship was cemented for life. He loved to cook for them too. They soon had a love of the Greek cuisine and the culture also.

Once qualified, Mr Marsh had promised that he would provide funding for them to set up their own business and would in return, take a small percentage of their profits. He had many contacts in the business so they were inundated with work from the very beginning. They soon had to employ new staff too. The business went from strength to strength in a very short time.

The years passed and Mr Marsh passed away peacefully in his sleep one autumn morning. His wife passed away within that same year. Their children inherited the land and the manor house. Sheila was delighted to find that she had inherited a huge amount of capital, as had Harry. They decided to invest some of it in the business and were looking at purchasing their own property where they could raise their family.

Life continued as normal and the family continued to work the land and to love the life they had. Sheila's mother and father enjoyed good health and Charlie became head grounds man. They were in touch on a regular basis and always happy to see one another. The two elder boys were by now married and settled too. Sheila's mother loved being a grandmother and loved the richness of their simple lives.

Part 3

Chapter Eighteen

The Sound Bath was very relaxing to Elizabeth. Walking into the room, Sheila and the twins were welcomed with hugs and smiles from everyone. It was obvious that they were well liked and well thought of too. She watched as she could see the pride in their eyes, as they turned to introduce her to the rest of the group.

"Well, we can see where your Mother gets her good looks from boys...you've obviously exceeded yourselves." Their delight that she was here with them was so infectious, she caught herself smiling and laughing with everyone, as though she had known them forever.

The boys had their little yoga mats to lie down on and their cushions and blankets. Watching them settle in so easily, Elizabeth once again felt that now familiar twinge in her heart centre. They were obviously looking forward to the session. She too was welcomed with hugs if she preferred them rather than just a simple handshake, or maybe just a smile. Never had she met such welcoming folks. Perhaps the word she was looking for was love. There was evidently so much love in that one room.

The boys took her mat from her and laid it down upon the floor placing Grandma, then Will, then her and then Ben by the wall closest to the window.

"You'll hear the birds outside in the trees mum too, by being here, it's our favourite spot" Ben advised.

They told her to snuggle down and advised with a huge grin on their faces, that there was to be 'No snoring.' They all giggled as Annie rang the chimes, advising that she would be starting in a couple of minutes.

"Good morning everyone and welcome to you, new and old alike, especially Elizabeth. I will be playing a variety of musical instruments; whistles, flutes, chimes, xylophone, tubular bells, singing bowls and possibly others too as I am guided by my intuition. These sounds will encourage the movement of each cell in turn and will re-balance the chakras. You might want to sleep, or simply offer an intention to The Universe, if you have a decision or a challenge upcoming. I advise lying down, rather than sitting, as the chakras will then be in line with the spine, although it is a personal choice and you should each follow your own body's intuition and feelings, as to how and where to position yourselves. If you feel more comfortable placing your hands upon the area around the heart through the meditation then that's what you should do.

The bathing of sound has been used for many centuries and I hope you will find it peaceful, calming, relaxing and inspiring too. The bath will take about an hour and I will sound the gong at the end, gradually building up the sound to bring you back into the moment, gently and easily."

Elizabeth made a mental note to ask Sheila later just what Annie meant. No sooner had the thought left her mind when Annie explained;

"Often the soul journeys to other realms and travels to seek Higher Wisdom from its origins or Source. Some of you call it One-Ness or God, or simply The Collective or The Universe."

Her passion was clearly evident, as she continued to explain;

"As the cells vibrate it encourages the lymph to circulate far more easily. This will release toxins from the blood and lymphatic system. This often means that many of you will need to pee frequently following the session."

At this point the boys let out a little giggle. She further advised;

"Listen to your body's wisdom for the next two or three days. It is essential that you drink water – preferably the filtered kind, in order to alkalise the blood and maybe also take a magnesium supplement too, which would encourage regeneration and rejuvenation of the cells. Some of you may have an amazing influx of energy, vitality and inspiration, whereas others might need more rest and relaxation. I have even known some people sleep for a full eighteen hours, after a sound bath healing session."

Several of the group quickly wandered off to the toilet, whilst their little foursome snuggled into their soft, cuddly blankets. Elizabeth did wonder what she would feel like when she awoke. She was rather surprised that others felt the need to pee so urgently, before the session began. She felt so much comfort at having her little family so very close to her. Even the love from Sheila was tangible, now more than ever.

As everyone returned and settled again, Annie started with a Native American Indian flute and then moved through to use the other instruments, as she had previously stated she would.

As Elizabeth closed her eyes, her thoughts drifted back in time. She was now reminding herself that she had once called Sheila a 'Witch Bitch.' As she remembered those thoughts of her old self, whom now she was really beginning to feel quite sorry for, she drifted into a faraway place. She had been small-minded, bigoted, cruel, judgemental and outright nasty. Little did she know that she was already well on the way to her inner path of compassion and forgiveness, forgiveness for herself and her own actions. She had heard over the years of others who had experienced this and it had often been said that *this is thought to be one of the hardest lessons which we will ever learn as a human being.* Those were her last thoughts before she drifted off into a deep and powerful meditation.

Chapter Nineteen

For the next few days following the Sound Bath, Elizabeth was amazed at how much lighter, healthier and better she felt. People had commented that 'she glowed' and looked wonderful. She thought Annie was a little crazy when she had mentioned that some folks might want to sleep more. Little had she known just how true it was to be! On the journey home, she had struggled to keep her eyes open. She was also bursting for yet another pee. So surprised was she, at the actual volume of water she released when they returned to Sheila's home.

Although lunch was already prepared in the kitchen, she had excused herself as she had to nip upstairs 'for a quick 50 winks' she said. Sheila nodded to the boys and they both followed their mother upstairs and tucked her up in the duvet. They snuggled into her, one behind and one in front of her chest, as they both somehow managed to stroke her long, wavy dark hair.

"I love you both so dearly boys and I'm so very sorry for my previous rat-bag self. Thank you for your forgiveness and your kindness. I love you."

Never had she experienced so much loving kindness and peace. She felt complete for the first time in her life. Together with those thoughts and her ever-opening heart, within seconds she was drifting off to that faraway place again.

She had slept for four solid hours. Upon awakening she knew that she hadn't even moved a tiniest amount. How the boys had managed to leave without waking her, was a miracle. Whilst asleep, Will had brought her a full pint glass of water and left it with a note on the bedside cabinet. Half dozed she opened the note which very simply said:

'I love you mummy and Thank You for being my mummy.'

Gratefully drinking the water, she sat in bed as she tried to become more awake. They had kindly opened the windows for her too and drawn the curtains, so that she could remain asleep, without the direct sunlight shining in her face.

As she raised herself up on the pillows further, she realised that she needed to pee yet again. Grateful for the en-suite, she saw that Sheila had placed some fresh flowers in the bathroom for her. Their fragrance seemed to fill the whole room and she had said

"Thank you" out loud before she realised and recognised her own voice. The next words she uttered were

"Kindness, loving kindness," once again the lips had moved without her mindful effort, or minds awareness. She still felt dozy and thought she would just sit in bed for a few more minutes before joining them all in the garden. She could hear their laughter and Sheila's gentle humming too. Once again Elizabeth drifted off to sleep to the comforting sounds and the general atmosphere of the peace, the comfort of the bed, the bedroom, the house and the garden all eased her mind, body and soul.

It was a further two hours later when she finally made her way into the garden. By now it was evening dinner and the boys were already half way through their meal. Sheila and the twins welcomed her as she was about to sit at the table. The patio set was laid out with a place for her and another place was laid. She was not aware of any visitors? Mind you she had been in bed for almost half of the day.

Sheila brought out the salad and roasted vegetables. Elizabeth suddenly felt very hungry indeed. As she ate the beautiful food, she listened to her sons telling her about their day's adventures. They had painted some pictures for her and Daddy too. They had watched one of their favourite films and had played in the grass collecting insects for their bug garden. She listened intently and was pleased that they had enjoyed their day. That familiar feeling arose once more in her chest too.

The food tasted lovely and Elizabeth realised how much she appreciated everything Sheila had done for her. She appreciated her sons and their love for perhaps the very first time. She appreciated being able to dine outside in the open air and really loved the simplicity of her son's sharing their stories with her.

"Thank you Sheila that was truly amazing and just what I needed." She thanked Sheila and helped tidy things away.

The boys settled into the lounge area. They loved this old house and they had a special playroom too where they could paint, colour, play with their model railway, their cars or Lego. After their evening meal they knew that they had an hour's quiet time before their bath, then story time and bed as they were tucked in for the evening. Sheila had always held this routine for her children, so it seemed natural to continue it with her grandchildren. They knew her well enough to know her boundaries and barriers. Usually by this time of day she was shattered anyway. Their wind down time allowed her to wind down too! Being a Grandma could be hard work at times.

As they listened to the boys playing quietly, Sheila explained;

"Ted is on his way, he often calls in whilst the boys are here."

She watched Elizabeth's face, looking for the usual signs that she was upset or stressed; the rolling of the eyes, tension in the shoulders or screwing up of the facial muscles. She was well aware that this young woman had grown so much in both emotional and spiritual wisdom in the last few days, though she was cautious on behalf of her son.

Their divorce had been relatively easy though Sheila had known right from their first encounter that they would be married, settle down and have a family. She also knew her son's heart would be well and truly broken, if not shattered by this woman. Being a parent hadn't been easy at all, watching him lose his father, then his marriage and his normal family life. Yet, throughout this time she had remained patient and as non-judgemental as possible towards them both. Never had she ever said anything negative about Elizabeth, especially not in front of the twins.

Elizabeth gave away no sense of tension, nor discomfort when her ex-husband Ted was mentioned, none of the usual signs were anywhere to be seen. Sheila breathed a sigh of relief and trusted that Elizabeth would be at ease in the presence of Ted. Just as she finished the breath, the door opened and seconds later her son entered the room holding Will and cuddling Ben into his right leg. As soon as he sat down, both were sat in their usual positions, Ben to the right and Will to the left. He bounced both of them about, whilst his mother handed him a cuppa.

He had noticed Elizabeth and smiled across at her. Sheila watched on, keen to see that these two were comfortable in the same room, particularly when they were in her house and the company of her dear grandsons. The ease between them was clearly obvious, if not a nice and welcome surprise.

The boys continued to tell daddy about their day and what they had been doing. Elizabeth smiled over at him and their sons. As the boys went to gather their artwork that they had made for him earlier, he smiled at Elizabeth.

"You look really well Elizabeth and you actually have a glow about you."

Inwardly he had seen that glow before when she was pregnant with the twins. He felt his heart sink at the thought, that she might be pregnant to another guy.

"I have felt amazing since the Sound Bath and Sheila has made me most welcome for the past couple of days. We have all thoroughly enjoyed ourselves."

As Ted watched her, her eyes seemed brighter, her body language more open and even her voice was lighter too. Almost everything about her had changed and the woman that had caused him so much pain in the past was sitting right here at the same dining table, where she had previously sulked and whinged at him, often in front of his whole family.

As if reading his thoughts, she was about to explain everything that had happened since she had caught sight of that falling star only three nights earlier. Just as she opened her mouth to speak, the twins stormed into the room, with their artwork for their father.

"This is amazing, how clever you are, I love it and will pin it up once I arrive home later." They looked across at Sheila, to ask if it was okay to take him into the garden too to see their bug garden. Without the needs for words, she nodded and they knew he would love it.

Sheila and Elizabeth sat quietly with their own thoughts, whilst they listened to the laughter and the screams. Will had obviously picked up a caterpillar, which Ted really wasn't too keen on. Sheila moved to pop her arm around Elizabeth's shoulder and in turn, Elizabeth wrapped her hand over Sheila's. The silence between them was a peaceful one, though short lived as the boys soon returned with their father.

Ted settled down with his cuppa again and Sheila said she would nip upstairs to run the boys their bath. Ted was still surprised by how well Elizabeth looked and at how comfortable they were to be in the same room together, after all these years. This was totally unfamiliar territory.

Usually he had bathed the boys when they were married and usually he bathed them whilst they were here too. Yet, when he and his sons were out of the room, the boys had explained;

"Mummy has been in our den, she loved it daddy. She even came to the Sound Bath with us and she let us snuggle right up to her without shouting. We have also been reading to her too."

Now he wasn't sure whether she would actually want to bathe them before bed. The change in Elizabeth was obviously making a huge difference to them all.

Chapter Twenty

Once the boys were settled and Ted had eaten, they all sat together in the snug. It was a lovely warm evening and the windows were still open, allowing in the welcome cool, evening breeze. The view from this room was so lovely and the three of them all agreed that its beauty provided them with so much to appreciate. They chatted about the architect who had been a wonderful friend to Will and Sheila for many years.

"How is Alexander mum? Have you seen him lately?" Ted enquired.

"Not recently, no dear, although I believe he has a birthday celebration coming up soon. Maybe I ought to call in on him and have lunch, or at the very least, a walk in the park with him." Sheila said.

"He's a good man mother and I know he misses dad such a lot, especially since he was widowed too."

"Yes, you're right, I'll give him a call tomorrow." Sheila made a note in her diary and Elizabeth watched her smile whilst she did so. It was obvious that she had a genuine affection for this man.

The conversation drifted comfortably to the change in Elizabeth, in so many ways. Ted felt very comfortable asking her about how she was feeling and how she was coping with so many new experiences. As she recalled the evening of her split from Robert to him, she was quite open about the incident and how upon her return home, she had seen a falling star and was guided to make a wish. Since then 'she had slept for England' and had had this incredible pain frequently in her heart centre.

"That's your heart centre opening" said Ted, as she looked directly from him and then to Sheila.

"Yes, that's what your mum kept telling me and giving me reassurances that all was well."

"It can be very painful, even though it might only be momentary" he continued.

Sheila watched, pleased to see them getting along so well after everything that had gone on previously. She had been pleasantly surprised watching Elizabeth open like a rose which was beginning to bloom. She knew it was an honour to share this precious time with her, whilst her spiritual journey was beginning.

"Why is it painful," Elizabeth was keen to know and understand what was happening to her.

"The heart has an intelligence all of its own. Most people live in their head and believe that what they are taught by society, such as religion, politics, social media, etc., is right. They never question what they are conditioned to believe. Yet the heart has a 'knowing' of its own and 'feels' what's right. That's why, whenever you used to request my opinion on something and ask, what do you think Ted, my reply would always be what do you feel?"

Elizabeth thought back to the days when she would often seek his opinion. Yet would rarely act on his advice. She was merely looking to *impress, rather than feel for the right or most appropriate outcome* in situations, dilemmas and through challenging times. For the first time in their *togetherness, she was actually really listening and really beginning to comprehend what he was saying to her.* She had indeed missed out on so much and knew that she had caused him so much pain throughout those years. She was now beginning to understand just how hard he had tried to assist her *to lose the dis-ease to please* and yet here she was finally grasping the *concept of listening to her own heart. Finally she was beginning to understand that all the answers she would ever need were already inside of her. She was finding her own inner truth, guidance and wisdom.*

Seeing the sadness and regret in her eyes, he reached over to place his hand over hers. Without the need for words, as they looked into one another's eyes, a deep peace and apology was communicated and acknowledged.

"Would you like me to continue?" he asked gently. She nodded as her eyes began to tear up.

"The physical body is the house for the soul. The soul is what connects us to *all things* and obviously to each other too. The soul needs to communicate through our physical body and does this through the chakras. We receive and transmit energies and emotions through them. These are energy vortexes which are situated at a variety of points on the body. They look very much like funnels and the base of each one of the funnels is situated on the spinal column.

The Earth rotates at 7.56 Hertz which is a frequency of energy. A Hertz is a revolution per second. Therefore, in order to anchor the soul into the body, the first of the seven chakras is based at the spine. This vibrates at 7.56 to up to 7,500Hz. Then the next chakra is situated at the sacral centre near the belly button, the next is the solar plexus and then the heart centre. The heart's frequency is between 25,000- 40,000 Hz, so now you can see just how much energy is awakening there as you are listening and using that wisdom."

Elizabeth listened intently and thought about how often he had chatted previously with friends and family members about the chakras. Never before had she even wanted to listen or comprehend. How sad that she had missed out on all this wisdom. She was entranced by this man and his wisdom, now that she was finally listening. Experiencing it was another matter.

Ted left her to her thoughts for a moment, allowing her time to process what he was saying. As he looked at her, she nodded and he continued.

"The heart is the fourth chakra and is situated between the three earth chakras, those which I have just explained to you, and the upper three centres." He then pointed to the throat, the third eye and the crown above the head. As he continued to explain;

"These are known as the upper centres. These are linking the soul to its Source, The Universe, God-Head, or whatsoever people would like to refer to it as". He paused there once again, to ensure she was with him and comprehending what he was saying.

"As the heart centre opens, the upper three chakras begin to activate and then we can connect to The Universal Wisdom or Universal Consciousness, as it is often referred to. These centres allow and provide us with our intuition, a deepening wisdom and assist us in finding our true passion and divine purpose. Most people remain in the material world and the physical realms, believing only what they see, hear and occasionally feel from others. Often they ignore their own intuition and their heart centre's wisdom, at a huge detriment to themselves. It is almost as though a part of them dies. This is why over half of patients who have a heart attack, do not present with any physical pathology at all. They have no congenital problems, neither do they have a cholesterol problem. The medical profession obviously cannot explain these and many other things." Again he paused and watched her body language before he continued;

"Just imagine a child who is repeatedly ignored by its parents, teachers, or siblings. Eventually they will withdraw from others and become quieter and quieter. They will learn to expect not to be heard and not to be listened to. This then becomes normal to them. They will often disregard others and begin to ignore others, thinking that this is the only way to behave. Again law of attraction will bring more of the same and it soon becomes a vicious circle of not being heard and not being able to listen to others. In the same way, we deny our heart centre's instincts and knowing. It then becomes a habit through repetition. We all know how hard it can be to break habits.

So, this is why your heart centre is painful, because you are finally listening. It's finally being heard and acknowledged and as such it is moving much more quickly. The painful discomfort you feel is the chakra wheel spinning, releasing the old you and expanding. The chakra is spinning faster and faster the more you listen. Imagine a centrifuge gaining speedy rapidly, as the speed increases it throws out things which have been weighing it down...those things which no longer belong in the vortex, old habits, conditioned behaviours, sadness, grief, to name but few.

You could also liken it to an old classic, vintage car that has not been used for some time, that's been neglected and left to rot in a shed. It might be covered in dust, rust and cobwebs, not to mention goodness knows what else. It will need a whole heap of tender, loving care to get it to its' original state. Commitment too is important, as whilst the repair work gets underway, it will be easy to wonder whether or not it's worth the time and the effort. Just imagine the result though once that car is restored to its former glory, all sparkly and the engine sounding healthy."

Whilst Ted continued, Elizabeth was wondering if this is why people had said 'she was glowing'.

"Most people get hurt in life. The obvious things are relationships and yet often we are discontented with our parents in the beginning. We might be compared to siblings, or might not be academic, or sporty enough to think that we are accepted. Our education system leads us to believe that we are not good enough if we cannot manage to achieve straight A's. We are encouraged to be competitive once we go to school. Often children as young as four begin to do tests. This creates separation and the need to prove oneself from a very early age. Obviously there are many wise teachers out there who do their best to teach children manners, morals and principles, also teaching team-building skills to compensate for the formal education systems lack of common sense and wisdom. You might call it control or propaganda.

So, I'm sure you can imagine that a child who is finding they cannot perform academically already begins to feel left out and separate at such a delicate stage in their life. It affects their confidence, feelings of security and many other things, generally leaving the child to grow up feeling more and more uncomfortable within themselves. Those that do achieve academically feel under constant pressure to keep achieving. Many who achieve academic prowess usually do so at quite a cost to their personal relationships. They struggle to have relationships with themselves and often few have common sense. Our whole society is led to believe success is built on academic and financial status. Yet we are desperate for practical people like brick-layers, electricians and carpenters to name but few. I love the quote by Einstein;

'The intuitive mind is a sacred gift and the rational mind is a faithful servant.

We have created a society that honours the servant and has forgotten the gift.'" At this point Ted paused.

"Success really should mean being fulfilled and following our hearts. Working at our relationships and finding a career which we love. I personally believe that it means bringing our children up to have common sense and teaching them to understand the wisdom of their own hearts. Asking them what they feel is right and what they would like to do in any given situation, especially important, when they are deciding what career they might like to follow. We should all be encouraged to follow our creative passions such as singing, dancing, paintwork, craftwork and many others. Often these are removed from the school syllabus, in preference of academic subjects.

Religions are often based on fear. We must please God in order that we can arrive at the pearly gates and get into heaven. Otherwise, the alternative is hell. Often people are taught that if they have been naughty or bad, they have sinned and therefore are not good enough to stand before God. These are all ways of separating us from the truth. Our truth. We then learn to judge ourselves, this becomes a habit, which can be incredibly hard to drop. By judging ourselves of course, we then judge others too. Law of attraction is at play in everything we do, the more we judge, the more we are judged. The more fear that we experience, the more fear we will create too. They keep us in fear, rather than in a state of peace and love. *Fear is the one thing which will definitely destroy love."* Ted finished talking and became reflective within the comfort of his parent's home.

She was beginning to see just how much of her life had been fear-based. When he explained that 'fear is the one thing which will definitely destroy love', she wondered how he had put up with her for so long. She felt sorry for him.

For the first time, she understood that the reason her parents had attended church every Sunday was to impress others and because they were terrified of dying. They had been conditioned to accept fear. The alternative was that they would go to hell. This led them to believe that they were Holier than others and thus better people. Yet, by fearing hell and focusing upon that, they were failing to live. The fear of dying was actually killing the joy within them. Bitter sweet irony indeed.

Ted noticed the sadness in her eyes and he felt it too. He had known her for so many years after all. He paused whilst she reflected and was beginning to fill in the gaps of her life and her previous existence. That's all it was she thought, an existence. She hadn't lived, rather she had created one drama after another. Her parents had led her to believe that she was better than most of the other children in the village, simply because they were of good stature at church and in the community.

Giving her plenty of time to process her thoughts, he continued when she once again nodded across the room to him. This was making so much sense. It was truly mind-blowing to her.

"Many people enter into a relationship thinking or feeling that it won't work out. Being aware of law of attraction means that that is in fact exactly just what they will create! Fear of being hurt leads us to close the heart centre. By the time we are old enough to experience intimate relationships, so much hurt has occurred in so many people, that they simply accept that fear and hurt really are what life is all about. People are taught what they should or should not do, how they should or should not behave and of course now with social media too in the mix, the pressure is ever increasing.

Being in the material world means that people are never satisfied, rarely happy and often discontented. They continually search for *satisfaction outside of themselves* in material things like wealth and status in the community. *They seek acceptance from society and others, without first seeking it in themselves.* As I said, the answers lie *within ourselves* and opening the heart centre is one sure way of beginning the journey to *finding your own truth*, rather than being forced to accept someone else's truth."

Elizabeth thought back to the times when she had thought that she always had to look great, wear fashionable items and accessories, that she must always wear perfect make-up too. She now realised that Ted really had loved her without any of those masks. The realisations she was making and experiencing as she was finally joining the dots, felt like a tornado hitting her. Watching her facial expression, Ted could see that she understood.

"You are finally on your way towards freedom" Ted smiled, obviously delighted.

"That's why I was such a bitch to you and our boys too. To you Sheila *and really to myself*. I'm truly sorry. Looking to the material world and looking to please others and impress others all the time has certainly taken its toll on me. I realise now that there was never a need to impress you, you simply saw the good within me and knew that I'd get to this point in my own time. I've really learnt the hard way. At least now I can begin to repair the damage by building on my relationships. *Not to mention that now I can begin to have a relationship with MYSELF."*

Sheila and Ted both looked at Elizabeth and once again without words, both expressed their delight at her understanding and comprehension. The three of them laughed whole-heartedly as Elizabeth said

"Better late than never then."

One thing that stayed with Elizabeth from that night was knowing that she was never judged for her previous actions. For the first time in her life, she had realised her wrong-doing and yet was able to be comfortable and at ease with it. By actually being accepted, she was now taking the first steps towards accepting herself and finding true freedom, freedom from her masks.

Chapter Twenty One

Elizabeth awoke the following morning to a knock on her bedroom door. She could hear the boys giggling to themselves. She shouted them to say;

"Come in" and they entered bringing her a tray of eggs benedict, which was her absolute favourite.

"Daddy made it for you. He slept in our room last night and woke up early to get ready for work. He is just leaving now and asked us to tell you to have a great day."

They had both climbed on the bed in a blink. She could hear his car on the driveway as he left. Once again her heart centre made its presence known to her.

"You're very kind for bringing this to me boys" she said. Just then Sheila popped her head around the bedroom door bringing her a cuppa.

"I'm just nipping out to the market Elizabeth, are you ok for a couple of hours? Would you like me to bring you anything? Would you like anything in particular for lunch?"

"No, I'm happy to let you decide thank you and yes, I'm fine here with these two munchkins. See you later and enjoy yourself too."

The boys were delighted to be called 'munchkins' and sat watching her as she ate her feast. As she tucked in heartily to her morning treat, the boys chatted about their den and she smiled whilst they all sat comfortably together feeling totally connected and contented.

The eggs were done to perfection, just as they always had been, she felt an intense gratitude towards Ted.

"Can we have a pyjama morning Mummy please? We can all snuggle together on Grandma's sofa watching a film like we do when we are here with Daddy."

Her smile was so large that they already knew the answer. They explained that they had already had their breakfast and would like her to watch a film with them. It was raining outside and they weren't too keen to play out in the rain. They asked if they might paint later, or even do baking with her. She simply agreed to everything and anything that was put forward, loving every single precious moment.

A few minutes later they were sorting through the children's films on NetFlix downstairs. They had all got drinks and Ben had brought in his favourite blanket, as they snuggled together.

"Frozen, Frozen, Frozen," they almost screamed when they found that particular film. As the music started, she thought of how often they had watched it whilst at her apartment. Yet she had always found something else to do, or someone to call. This would be the first time she would indeed, watch it all the way through and enjoy their company.

The film started with the men digging out the ice and working together, whilst encouraging a young boy to join them and learn their skill. Encouragement and camaraderie indeed. Will and Ben sat quietly snuggled, one at either side of her. It wasn't long before Ben would scramble onto her knee. He made himself comfortable and she was aware that he was listening to her heartbeat, through her chest. Just how many times he had tried to cuddle her and she had rejected him, she didn't care to recount.

"Don't be sad Mummy, just enjoy the NOW" he said.

As she looked down at him, she wondered if he had known what she had been thinking. He was lying across her heart centre after all.

The film opened further with the two sisters; Elsa and Anna, enjoying magic as a gift. The *parents saw only the fear in the gift* of their daughter's magic and encouraged them to hide it, rather than learn to control and use it with wisdom. How strange that she had watched it before, in between watching over her boys, yet never seen the hidden wisdom. In the film, Elsa, the older sister, uses her magic to create a beautiful ice tower and can finally really be who she is, without fear. Those who do not understand the magic, destroy the tower, due to their fear of the unknown. The love her sister possesses for her, their family and friends is so profound and evident throughout the whole film. The younger sister a child of pure innocence and grace.

They laughed at the various points when the huge ice monster appeared in the film and Elizabeth jumped in her seat. They knew the film word for word. It was a definite favourite of theirs. Time with their mother was so precious to them. Each of the three of them knew that they had much to make up for. Today was indeed a great day and this was a great start to the day.

'Frozen' indeed, she thought to herself as she continued to watch the film, knowing now the power of her own fear. Reflecting upon how the younger sister refuses to allow fear to control and manages to focus on love instead, even up to the point where she herself is frozen ice.

Elizabeth thought that the ending was most clever as the words 'love thaws' rang through her head. Teds words too were going around and around in her head, *'fear is the one thing which will definitely destroy love.'*

She was crying at the end of the film. The boys hugged her more tightly, passed her the box of tissues and suggested they all have a snack together. They requested eggs with toasted soldiers for lunch. Later whilst watching them tuck in she knew that Sheila would soon be back too. She reached to check her phone, just as she heard a text come through. 'I'll be another hour or two, just bumped into an old friend. Help yourselves to whatsoever you like and I'll see you later. Love Sheila.'

The weather was beginning to brighten though the grass was still very wet. As they all tidied the kitchen and retired to play, she could feel her inner child showing herself and wanting to join in. The boys wanted to play with the model railway set they had in the playroom and paint too. The twins also asked to listen to their favourite music. Whilst they all played they sung at the top of their voices.

When Sheila returned, all she could hear was laughter and singing. A huge smile spread across her face as finally her grandsons could be at one with their mother. She was thrilled that Elizabeth could now find her own inner peace, rather than be forever searching for yet another mask, or material possession to hide behind.

The three of them hadn't heard Sheila return. She was busy in the kitchen putting away the shopping, when they heard the kettle whistle, signalling that it was boiling on the stove. They really had been singing so loudly! They all ran into the kitchen to see if they could help out. The boys always knew that she would have a treat ready for them. Sometimes she would make them a list of clues, rather like a treasure hunt, until they could seek out the treasure. Usually the treat was a gingerbread man or a lollipop, maybe an ice-cream or something creative to keep them occupied. They loved her clues and it usually didn't take them long to seek the so-called treasure.

Elizabeth helped with the remaining shopping, whilst the boys worked through the clues. It was the very first time she had ever helped in the kitchen. Another painful reminder of her past self. Yet, at the same time, she realised it was also a blessing. It was up to her to be open to learning, rather than fill herself with regret and remorse for her previous actions. She was learning more about The law of attraction daily and really did not wish to waste any more time on the past.

It wasn't long before they heard the twin's howls of delight from the hallway. They ran into the room each with a gingerbread man and a new activity colouring book filled with various puzzles and games too. They settled down at the table with a drink of fresh fruit juice. Once the gingerbread men were gobbled up, they were off to enjoy their new books. The playroom was silent, as they were engrossed in the various interests.

As she and Sheila settled over a cuppa, Elizabeth asked how she had enjoyed her morning. Once again she surprised herself with her consideration. Her former self never asked anyone how they were, she usually waited for someone to ask her how she was. She surprised herself further by noticing that she was actually listening intently and looking forwards to what Sheila would have to say. She found the conversation so easy after all these years and realised further, that the conversation was completely effortless. Despite previously feeling that Sheila had always blocked conversation, she understood that it had been her doing.

Once again it had been the law of attraction at play, as previously she had thought that no-one ever wanted to listen to her. Thus to gain their attention, she always had to impress them in some way, shape or form. Now she was beginning to put all these unfortunate habits behind her.

"I had gone to the market and was deciding whether or not to sit in the lovely new organic café, which has recently opened in the nearby square. I knew that you were all okay here and that I didn't need to rush back. Just as I was about to purchase a loaf of organic bread, I turned around upon hearing a familiar voice. It was our old family friend Alexander, the man Ted and I were chatting about last night. He asked me if I was busy, or would I like to sit and have a coffee with him in the newly opened café. He had been a wonderful friend to William and had been so supportive to all the family, throughout William's illness. I had promised to keep in touch at the funeral and it hadn't been too long afterwards that he too was widowed."

As Elizabeth listened she could feel the respect between Sheila and Alexander. Their friendship had obviously lasted several decades and she began to explain that they had all met at college. Sheila had been encouraged with her artwork and then been offered a sponsorship to an architectural college.

Elizabeth listened intently to Sheila, who suggested that as the food and service were really fabulous, they should do 'Ladies At Lunch' together soon. She was obviously thrilled to have caught up with her old friend too. Elizabeth was pleased to have been invited for lunch. 'Goodness how many things have changed for me in the last week' she thought to herself.

It was by now late Friday afternoon. Elizabeth was aware that Ted was due to have the twins this weekend and would be arranging to collect them in a few hours' time. Ted had clothes, shoes, coats and everything they needed at his place, so she was quite contented to stay here until his arrival.

Chapter Twenty Two

Spending the weekend alone was usually a real blast for Elizabeth. She was still in a relationship with Robert less than a week ago and they usually spent time together once his working week had finished. Now, here she was alone and was really missing her sons, even though they had only been gone for less than an hour.

For the first time ever, she sat and looked around her apartment. When they had divorced, Ted had suggested that she purchase a house, rather than an apartment. The boys would then have a garden to play in and she more space. So keen to impress others, she had opted for an apartment nearer to the city. After being in the countryside with Sheila for a few days, she realised now the essence of Ted's wise words. Looking around she saw everything through new eyes. The apartment was clinical and bland, *not homely in any way*. All the toys, artwork, children's books, teddies and games were always tucked away out of sight.

The whole place seemed empty and without life. Sheila's home oozed love. This place was nothing but a barren shell. As she went from room to room, nothing was out of place. Nothing was dirty and there was very little dust. It seemed as though no-one lived here at all. There was still a little laundry from the boys, yet everything else was spotless. Apart from one photograph, she had no 'clutter,' such as ornaments, or things of sentimental value or feeling either. Sheila's house was full of family photographs, artwork, wooden carvings and vases of beautiful flowers.

As she sat down, she looked around and began to visualise the place looking more homely. She was lucky enough to have money from the weekly maintenance and the divorce settlement, therefore, she didn't have to work. She had invested money weekly since the divorce and began to consider moving from here and maybe making a new start for her and her twin sons. She knew she would be looking at houses, rather than apartments. Reconnecting to Sheila's garden in her thoughts, she even thought about moving to the countryside. A property away from the city would be much cheaper and much more peaceful too. How strange she thought, that only a few days ago, she had loved the hustle and bustle of the city, whereas already she was feeling uncomfortable at the constant traffic and the noise pollution.

She decided to run herself a bath. Sheila had been kind enough to make a wonderful evening meal which they had all shared together, before she left. Now feeling really tired, she knew a bath would be a great place to rest easy and think of how she would spend her time wisely this weekend. She recognised that she was genuinely beginning to be grateful for everything she experienced. Even the simple things, such as hot running water and the lovely aromatherapy candle that Sheila had passed to her just as she was leaving. She got her nightshirt ready and looked through her favourite films, whilst the bath was running.

As she lay in the bath, with the scent of the candle lifting her mood more and more, her thoughts drifted to days long gone. Inevitably, she thought of Ted. Whilst they were married, he always made time for the boys. He was the one who always wanted to make time for them as a couple too. She was often busy with so-called friends, or on her phone. She was beginning to see that the cracks were already there in the marriage, well before his father was poorly. She was also recognising that he really had pulled out all the stops and tried his best, whereas she had failed to relate to herself, her sons and certainly, he had always been last on the list. She felt really sorry for Ted.

Trying to juggle work and family life was never an easy task. He would come home from work, often bedraggled and stressed, and yet always found the energy to pick them both up in his arms and provide them with hugs and kisses. He had had his own property business for years and was a very prosperous man. His business took up much of his time, though they managed family holidays and weekends away.

He was a really great businessman, well-respected and well-liked too. He had a well-earned reputation in his field. He always put his family first though and would happily delegate to his deputy managers, if the boys or Elizabeth were poorly. A good manager empowers his staff and he had definitely acquired that skill. His staff respected him, as did his clients and even his rivals in business.

Once his father became ill, finding time to manage that business too was a real problem. With very little support from Elizabeth, life was really taking its toll. He struggled further as his father had let quite a few things slip. William had been ill for a while before being diagnosed. Several projects were taking far longer to complete than they should have done and the cash-flow was greatly reduced as a result. Some of the staff were not pulling their weight and knew they were able to sneak away earlier than they should have at the end of the day. Ted was deeply saddened to see such a huge business depleted and in need of such intense restructuring to repair and restore it to its former glory.

Ted found it hard that his father wasn't available, nor able to discuss what needed to be resolved for the improvements to occur. Sheila had so much to deal with watching William deteriorate and had voiced her concerns to him some months ago. Neither of them had seen this coming though, neither the illness, nor the decline in the business. It was a huge shock on many levels.

Elizabeth realised that she had never spared a thought for Ted's well-being whilst they were together. He would come home looking absolutely shattered and on more than a few occasions he looked quite poorly, she thought. Never had she offered to run him a bath, or massage his shoulders. He was a much better cook than she was, so he had said that he was happy to cook for them. Running both businesses had taken its toll and often it would be so late when he arrived home, that he would simply collect a take-away on his way home.

Knowing he would be late home from work, Elizabeth fed the boys on ready meals and junk food as it was so much easier. McDonalds was a particular favourite, as they could play in the adventure playground, or the ball pond, whilst she had checked her messages and social media. She was a reasonably good cook and yet had allowed them to eat food poor in nutritional value, just to annoy Ted.

How often had she moaned at him for being late home, saying that she was really hungry? She was annoyed by his apparent lack of consideration, as she had wanted to eat earlier. As soon as he walked through the door most evenings, he would be greeted with her moaning about having to bathe the boys alone and put them to bed. He had always read them a story, even whilst they were tiny babies. She was so cross that she now had to continue the story habit, as he was too busy and would often only be home once they were already fast asleep and tucked up in bed. She even accused him of having an affair with his secretary. 'The blame game' was rife in her thinking throughout those months.

Now she was finally beginning to understand that he must have been under so much pressure and stress running both businesses. For the first time, whilst she reflected upon her actions, she realised how much sadness he must have been feeling about the inevitably of losing his father and having to watch his rapid deterioration. Then there was Sheila, who was obviously struggling to witness the demise of her husband too. Not once had she ever considered what they were going through.

How little time she had shown Joanne, Ted's sister who had idealised her dear father. Yet Joanne had always been so kindly towards her and the twins. Joanne had often offered to look after the boys and Elizabeth was always glad to have someone, anyone, take them off her hands. Previously she had collected the twins regularly and provided her with respite two mornings a week and one afternoon, since they were only a few months old. Had she ever thanked her?

Whilst William had been ill in the hospital and later the hospice, Elizabeth had been so pissed off that Joanne no longer took care of the boys. She had two boys herself and they would often really enjoy being with their older cousins. Needless to say, Elizabeth never offered to have all four children!

Recounting the months during William's illness and his deterioration, she also remembered the feelings of intense jealously, when they were altogether as a united family at the hospital. Elizabeth had felt like an outsider and felt surplus to requirements. Now she realised *that she had completely ostracized herself* and *had played the victim each and every day.* Now she could also see just how selfish she had been and what a complete bitch she thought to be honest.

She was beginning to realise that taking personal responsibility for her actions meant being aware of how she responded in any given situation. Making a promise to herself that from this day forward she would be more mindful of her actions was a huge step. She knew one thing for sure though, that despite everything, her in-laws had never judged her in any way. She could in no way at all, criticise them.

She recalled that often in the rows between her and Ted, most of which she had instigated, especially those leading up to her divorce from Ted, he had often said how 'closed, cold, disconnected and isolated' she seemed. He had felt that she was 'like a block of ice' and 'he couldn't get close to her.'

Elizabeth felt that if they were making love, then surely that in itself was closeness. She was now beginning to see just how wrong she had been all these years. As her thoughts drifted to Ted, she realised just how much immense patience he had had with her.

'Ignorance is bliss' she thought and decided to get out of the bath and retire to bed. She was beginning to comprehend the extent of all the hurt she must have caused Ted and his family. *'To love and be loved, is the greatest gift we can receive and experience in a lifetime.'* By now she was quite used to the voices and nudges of her spirit guide. Indeed, she wondered, had she had it all along and never realised? Her heart centre drew her attention once again. Reflecting upon her actions and allowing herself forgiveness were a huge part of her journey towards change and living a much more fulfilling life.

Elizabeth was certainly learning to forgive herself for the lack of respect she had shown herself and others. She was beginning to understand how precious time really is and just how often she had misused it! The time and patience that others had shown her over the years came to mind. Just how many people had tried to open her eyes and her heart to the truth of life and how to live? What would it have been like to understand and to live a fulfilling life previously? Where had she been up until recently? Was it really true that she had lost so much time? Would she be given these precious opportunities to make up for lost time in relationships?

For the first time ever, she understood just how lucky she was that she had time. Ted paid more than enough maintenance, in order that she did not need to work. If she had needed to work; maybe a forty hour week, she now considered just how tired and stressed she would be at the end of the day. She had always known that he would much prefer her to spend quality time with the boys, rather than time with boyfriends and so called 'friends.' Through these quiet reflections the revelations she was uncovering were potentially life changing. She knew she now had the courage to act upon them and she was wise enough to know that the results would be outstanding.

As her thoughts drifted to friendships, she realised for the first time that she had never really had a best friend. Now, she was beginning to understand why. *'Time is your greatest asset,'* she heard and she truly hoped she would be given the opportunity to make up for lost time. Already she was thoroughly enjoying her time, or rather quality time with her boys and with Sheila. Once again she experienced the familiar gripping pain. *'Forgive yourself for your unknowing.'*

There were so many things which she had ignored, throughout her thirty something years. One thing that was now clear to her, after her chats with Sheila and Ted, was how important her intuition was, or at least it should have been. All her life she had experienced Deja vu and a very strong intuition and yet had ignored her own most powerful feelings. Continuing with her reflections she recalled that she had a knowing when one of the women she worked with years ago had become pregnant. As she thought back she had known before the lady herself. There was another time when an older lady had a miscarriage.

It seemed to her now that throughout her whole life, she had been so determined to ignore her own soul and her feelings. In fact, she herself knew when she was pregnant that she was carrying twins, rather than a single pregnancy. She knew they were identical twin boys within a month of their conception. How many lies and untruths had she experienced? Lying in bed now, she tuned into her intuition. Just what was it showing her? One thing she did know for sure was that she would certainly be more open to listening.

Ted's words echoed inside her head; *'The intuitive mind is a sacred gift and the rational mind is a faithful servant. We have created a society that honours the servant and has forgotten the gift.'*

The tiredness descended and she surrendered with humility. She allowed herself to be forgiven by the powers that be above and realised that self-forgiveness is such a necessary part of life and living. Now Elizabeth understood more than ever why her heart centre was expanding and crying out for her attention.

As she lay in bed later that evening, she wondered if she would ever forgive herself as she drifted into a really deep, serene, peaceful sleep. Why was it always easier to be forgiven by another person, than it was to forgive yourself?

Chapter Twenty Three

The following morning she awoke to the sound of the traffic and the usual city hustle and bustle, rather than the quiet of the countryside and the birdsong. She was already really missing her boys. She also recognised that she did in fact miss Sheila too. She had always welcomed her in the mornings whilst she had stayed those few precious days and had obviously loved having her around.

As the thoughts of the previous evening ran through her head, she remembered that Sheila had suggested she try to connect with her own inner child – little Elizabeth. Maybe it was worth a try? Sheila was always so positive and encouraging. She said that just because something had always been that way, didn't mean that it couldn't be changed. Often people get used to cruelty, poverty or living with the lack of love. '*All things can change*' she would repeat regularly.

Could it be that because she had not received nurturing, she was denying her boys? Was it because it brought back too many painful childhood memories? Was it too late? Did she actually know how to nurture them? Was it possible to make up for all this lost time? Would she be able to learn maternal skills and nurturing skills from Sheila? Could her sons guide her? Her sons certainly seemed to be willing to be patient with her. They were more than happy to encourage her to play in their den, on the swings and in the sandpit too.

She had missed out on so much over the years and was beginning to understand for the very first time, that her own little girl had also missed out on fun and laughter. As she tried to recall a happy childhood memory, she thought about a church trip to a circus and remembered laughing at the clowns. She had been in awe of the elephants and frightened at the growl of the tigers. The combination of the bright lights, the smells of popcorn and the animals was overwhelming and breath-taking to a child of seven. As she recalled the event, she clearly recalled her mother's distaste at the animals and the noisy atmosphere too. Her father was off drinking at the bar with the other fathers in the group. Elizabeth was sat behaving and sitting up straight with her mother. She was certainly not allowed to pet the animals, nor play with the other children.

Concentrating further upon the scene, from so many years ago, she had realised as a child that her mother only seemed to brighten her mood rarely. It was usually when she was showing off to other people from the church. In particular the priest, or someone who was 'respected' in the community. She remembered that her parents never seemed to spend quality time together as a couple, they rarely spent *quality time* with her. How sad she thought that now she too, had very little understanding of *quality time*. Yet she knew that she had the impetus to learn and make the necessary changes. Was this also perhaps why she had had no awareness that she had needed quality time with her husband?

Her thoughts inevitably moved back to that morning only a few days ago, when she had fallen in the park. Would her inner child like a walk and maybe she would also like to feed the ducks too? She knew she had some sunflower seeds in the kitchen cupboard and thought to herself that now was as good a time as any.

Could Elizabeth bring herself to trust that this just might be true? What if? What if she could in fact connect to that inner child and in doing so, could understand herself more and thus understand her sons more? Supposing by connecting to 'Little Elizabeth,' it would assist in the healing process. She knew in her heart that by making these simple changes, the results would be wonderful. Surely it was worth a try at least.

Within minutes she was dressed and had had her usual fruit smoothie. The fridge was almost empty, so she thought she would visit the local market too, rather than do the on-line shopping. She packed the shopping bags into the Range Rover, so that when she returned from the park, she could travel to the local market hall.

As she walked towards the park, she took in all the architecture of the buildings in turn. She noticed each and every garden, the beautiful flowers and shrubs, trees and any garden ornaments too. It was clear to her that there were many things which she had previously ignored. Now she was appreciating the simple things in her everyday life.

Nearing the park she could hear children laughing and saw a family with a dog playing with a ball and a Frizbee too. She walked at a slower pace in order to pay more attention to their games and their conversations, without being too obvious and intruding on their space. She smiled as she listened to how easily their conversation flowed. She realised that they were simply being. It was effortless and they were in complete harmony. She was obviously trying too hard and realised that she just needed to be, allowing things to happen in their own time, rather than having huge expectations and unrealistic goals. This family had simply come out to enjoy the park. They had no agenda, no plans and seemed care-free. Maybe that was the answer itself? She listened to her intuition and knew it to be true.

She was nearing the duck pond and reached into her bag for the seeds. There were quite a variety of wildfowl here and she was thrilled to feed them. They quacked happily and she really could feel 'Little Elizabeth' enjoying herself thoroughly. It wasn't long before she had emptied the bag of sunflower seeds. She made a mental note to purchase some more and to bring her boys here. She thought of the Mediterranean man, who had helped and assisted her only a few days earlier too. Should she perhaps call on him and express her gratitude?

"Good morning, how's the ankle?" She turned around to see Alexander, the Mediterranean man smiling at her.

"Would you like a walk with an old man?" he suggested playfully.

"Yes please" she answered.

"I see that you're walking on it, without trace of a limp" he mentioned.

"Yes, it's been fine since that morning, I really wanted to come and show my appreciation. There's really no need, just a simple smile is gratitude enough." He beamed.

They walked around the pond and chatted about the park, its history and smiled with the children. They laughed along the path, watching the ducks slip on the mudded banks. He invited her for a cuppa and some breakfast if she preferred? She thought back to that delicious fruit salad and Greek yoghurt from the other morning. Without a moment's hesitation she had agreed. They sat out in the garden on the patio, as they had done previously and enjoyed the sunshine. He invited her inside, though they agreed that they both preferred the fresh air.

As he popped the kettle on, she admired the plants in the various pots and hanging baskets. It wasn't long before he appeared with a tray of goodies. Croissants, fresh fruit salad and yoghurt, a variety of jams too. What a treat she thought. He poured the tea and they tucked into the fruit salad and enjoyed the croissants too.

"I'm delighted that you are okay now. You certainly had taken quite a tumble last week. I remember you shed a few tears too. How do you feel now?" He was direct and his voice filled with compassion. She found herself being equally open and direct quite easily.

"To be honest, so much has happened in the last few days since we met. I was collecting my twins from my mother-in-law following our meeting and you had said 'Children just need to be nurtured.' I researched the word and found that over the coming days, I realised that I had not nurtured them at all. Ensuring that they were fed, watered, clean and tidy, certainly wasn't enough. When I collected them from Sheila's house, they were explaining to her that they didn't want to come home with me. They were obviously very upset that they had to leave her. Listening to them broke my heart open even more." The emotion in her voice was very touching.

"Sheila had always been kind to me and yet I had never seen it previously. She found me crying in the hallway, after overhearing their conversation. She invited me to stay over for the next few days and never before had I experienced such loving kindness. The following few days were a real eye opener. Spending time with her and my sons, just doing the simple things and spending time *with them, listening and being in the moment were truly wonderful.* I had never shown her any kindness at all. It was as though all that I had previously done was forgotten and was simply laid to rest. Even my ex-husband Ted, was kind with me when he came to see the boys.

We chatted easily and he explained that my heart centre was opening. It has been nothing short of a miracle to be honest. Ted has the boys this weekend, as we have been divorced for several years. Spending time alone at last night, I sat in the bath, reflecting on how badly I had treated him when we were married. I truly have made so many mistakes. He lost his father, William, several years ago and I failed to be supportive in any way. Goodness, how I wish I could turn the clock back."

Elizabeth had surprised herself at her openness and her ease of conversation. There was plenty of emotion in her voice and yet no 'crocodile tears.' Alexander just sat quietly and listened. What a difference in this young lady he thought. He had met Sheila in the market the day before and over a light lunch, she had explained that her daughter-in-law was staying with her. She told him that she was loving each and every moment. Sheila continued to say that she was pleasantly surprised when her and Ted were reintroduced too. They had a long conversation, about how Elizabeth had been thoroughly engaging with her boys, after all these years too. They had a good catch up and during the conversation, he had mentioned to her this young lady who had fallen in the park a few days ago. He told her that she had been crying and he had advised her about nurturing her family. He had trained in Reiki and Homeopathy, some years earlier. He explained his delight that the arnica had worked its magic so quickly. He explained to Sheila that he knew she would open up her heart centre, as she had soaked up the Reiki healing.

He sat with his thoughts, wondering whether or not to tell her, that he actually knew of how much this young, delightful woman had always meant to her extended family. 'What a tangled web we weave,' he thought to himself.

He had come over to England when he was just 19 years old. His father had a great business in architecture, building houses across the whole of Greece. He wanted his son to follow in his footsteps, regardless of what his son's wishes were. He sent him over here with very little awareness of the language or the culture. He struggled to cope with the cold weather and especially the rain. He had felt like a fish out of water and yet, by some miracle, he had been welcomed into the architectural college by two wonderful people; Sheila and William.

They spent so many hours with him, helping him to learn the language, cope with the weather and settle into the culture too. The three of them became great friends and they even worked together on many projects, before they decided to go into business together. Alexander had retired early, as he wanted to spend time with his family. His daughter had married a Greek and would be living mainly in Athens, so he wanted to spend time with them and his wife.

Since then, he had become a sleeping partner and still had huge investments with them. However, when William's health deteriorated very rapidly, he received a phone call from a most desperate Ted and he had agreed to return part time, to oversee many of the outstanding builds. Ted's father was a magnificent architect and built homes for the very wealthy. He was able to work on restorative projects too, with the help of Sheila's brother, Harry.

They all got along and Alexander was close to Harry as he had worked abroad and spoke several different languages. He loved

Greece and the culture and had in fact worked with his father on certain projects, often in an advisory capacity.

They were sat in a comfortable silence enjoying breakfast when the telephone rang interrupting their thoughts. He excused himself, whilst he answered the call in the lounge. As Elizabeth's continued eating her breakfast, her thoughts wandered to Sheila's kindness and her gratitude shone through.

Alexander received a phone call from Sheila.

"Hello" Alexander answered.

"Good morning Alexander, how are you? I'm wondering if you would like to come to a birthday party soon and meet the family again, sooner, rather than later. Ted has missed you and thought it would be a wonderful idea to meet?" Sheila asked.

"Thank you once again for the wonderful lunch we shared yesterday." She continued.

He wondered whether to suggest they should all meet up today, the three of them.

"I have a surprise for you. Are you free for lunch later today?" Alexander asked.

"Yes I'm feeling a little lost and even a little lonely, after having the company of Elizabeth and her grandsons for the previous few days. Yes, what a marvellous idea, that would in fact be a fabulous treat indeed."

With a huge grin on his face, as he put down the receiver, he asked Elizabeth what she had planned for the rest of the day. She stated that she needed to restock the fridge and was planning to go to the market hall. She explained that her plans were quite flexible though. One thing she had learnt over the last few days, was to be in the moment and be in harmony with the universe. Going with the flow was a whole new concept and seemed quite exciting to her.

"Would you like to come with me for lunch, my treat of course? I know this wonderful café and I have a feeling you'd like to meet a most dear and treasured friend of mine." She agreed within a second or two, after listening to the advice from her heart.

Chapter Twenty Four

Alexander parked his car in the local car park. Throughout the morning their conversation was easy. He asked her about her sons and her intentions, as she had mentioned earlier that she had thoughts of leaving her apartment. He listened, without having explained to her at this stage that he was in the property market. He had just the right house in mind too. He smiled to himself, as she described exactly what she thought would be a perfect home for herself and her sons. He had overseen the building of this particular house and despite the fact that it was perfect for a family, no-one had moved in.

It had been built for a very wealthy family, who had properties all over the globe. Their international business was widely successful and although huge within the UK, they just simply preferred warmer climates. When Mr Brookes visited England, his family would stay in another country and he would either stay in a local hotel, or with friends.

Listening to Elizabeth describe the layout of the house, how many bedrooms, reception rooms, the kitchen design and even the bathrooms, it was as though she herself had drawn the plans! Having been aware of the Universal Laws of Synchronicity for more years than he cared to recall, he smiled, in deepest appreciation, knowing that all was unfolding in perfect timing.

The cafe was simply called 'In Harmony.' Simple enough and obviously a significant statement within the title, meaning that the food was organic and was therefore grown 'in harmony.' This was just as it should be, rather than with man's interference. Genetically modified foods were not healthy in many ways, not to mention that the bees struggled too.

They were seated at a most beautiful wooden table with lovely hand-made wooden chairs. The selection of different fruit juices and herbal teas was quite amazing she thought. Their drinks were ordered, whilst they waited for his mystery guest. Looking around she was captivated and admired the wall hangings and pictures. They were placed on most of the walls and the attention to detail here was truly remarkable. The whole place felt homely and had a certain peace. As the aromas that were wafting from the kitchen touched her senses further, Elizabeth really hoped that the owners reaped the rewards for their work. She felt that they certainly deserved it. Light classical music played and all in all, it really was a place of 'harmony.' Whilst in here, it seemed the rest of the world didn't even exist.

Just as their drinks arrived, Sheila entered through the door. Alexander had been keeping an eye out for her, as she had text to say that she was just parking the car. Elizabeth was startled and delighted at the same time. She had been missing her after all, even though it was only less than twenty four hours since they had been together. The two ladies laughed, as Sheila had also been told that he wanted to introduce her to his 'mystery guest'. They hugged and smiled, laughing at Alexander and how the set of circumstances over the previous days had brought them here. Elizabeth was so delighted that she didn't feel the need to ask how they actually knew each other, she merely *delighted in the moment.*

Alexander had ordered Sheila's drink, knowing that she was on her way, so they all sat and chatted about how wonderful it was to be able to put these jigsaw pieces together. The events of the last few days had been awakening and wonderful for Elizabeth. It was clearly obvious to her that both Sheila and Alexander had so much in common and the mutual respect was touching to see. She listened to them as they shared their conversations from the previous day, neither knowing at that time, that they were chatting about Elizabeth. Clearly they were delighted that she had an understanding of the changes that were happening to her, her ability to receive at last was flowering too.

Elizabeth knew that she had turned a huge corner in her life, through her many reflections she was already learning so much about herself. She had always been concerned previously with controlling and planning her life and her children's. Now, here she was, just *allowing it all to unfold, with an awareness for the very first time of universal trust.* She realised just how hard it had all been previously, thinking that she had to control absolutely everything and that the main way in which to do that was through impressing others! No wonder she was always tired and cranky. Now she was at least beginning to find her inner peace and inner wisdom, which would guide her to exactly where she needed to be.

Once they were seated and the drinks had arrived Elizabeth began to explain her thoughts:

"I have chatted to Alexander earlier that I am thinking about moving from the apartment. I think the boys would benefit hugely and I just want peace, rather than the hustle and bustle of city life."

She went on to describe the house design that she desired for the second time that morning. Listening to her description, Sheila and Alexander looked across at each other and laughed. Elizabeth curled her brow, wondering what was so funny.

“I have the perfect property and I suggest that after lunch we nip to my office for the keys and then take a look. Are you both free this afternoon?” Alexander asked.

All three of them were looking forward to sharing the experience together of viewing a potential new home for a woman who was definitely spreading her wings.

Lunch was ordered and it wasn’t long before it was served. Elizabeth thought it was truly divine. Served with freshly made bread, delicious organic butter and salad dressings to die for, they knew they were in for a real treat. They all loved their individual meals and were thrilled by the service too. Could they manage a pudding or a dessert too? Sheila suggested that as they were celebrating, they should buy cakes to celebrate at the house later. The decision was made and they all agreed, although choosing which cakes was a little more difficult, as the choices were amazing.

Alexander kindly paid for lunch and they all felt that it would be the first of many meals together. He offered to drive and both women were seated comfortably in his Mercedes. When he parked outside William’s old office, Elizabeth looked confused. Then when he walked in and was greeted with utmost respect from the staff, she was even more confused. He obviously knew his way around and gathered up the said keys, within two minutes. She was quite surprized and taken aback. Alexander and Sheila just allowed her the time to join the dots together, whilst they prepared to answer any questions that she might have.

“So you’re Alexander The Great” she almost stammered.

"You have known Sheila and William for years and helped Ted whilst William was so ill. I'm well and truly gob-smacked, what a surprise indeed and such a small world."

"I only realised a little earlier this morning. When we originally met you asked me my name, though when I asked you, you failed to reply. I just put it down to the shock of the fall. Thus, neither of us had any knowing of our connection. We had breakfast inside the house and if you had come indoors you would no doubt have spotted the photographs of William, Sheila, Ted and the twins. I have often met your sons and Ted has given me several photographs over the years." Alexander explained.

He had always been like an uncle to Ted and was known as 'Great Uncle Alexander The Great' to the boys.

Laughing, Elizabeth excused herself whilst she visited the ladies room. Whilst washing her hands, she noticed a pretty picture frame on the wall and read the following whilst she allowed her excitement about viewing the house to grow. It was titled;

'Do you want to spread your wings and fly?

It happened one day that a small boy did observe a butterfly starting to emerge from its cocoon. Small was the hole it had fashioned therein as it sought to break free. Great was the excitement of the boy. But then did this excitement turn to concern, for the butterfly was struggling with all its might and yet seemed to advance not. It appeared to be entirely stuck. Fearing that the butterfly might perish, the boy ran to fetch a pair of scissors – though he did walk back, in accordance with the commandment of his mother – and with great care he cut a larger hole in the cocoon.

The butterfly was free! But the body of the butterfly was sorely swollen and its wings were shrivelled and small. It could not fly; it did crawl upon the ground.

And for the rest of its days, which were not great in number, it remained so. The boy knew not that the struggle doth push the fluid of its body into its wings. Without that struggle, it would never fly.

The Butterfly

Dale Stafford The Book of Job'

Chapter Twenty Five

The drive was a little over an hour. The property was situated in a little hamlet, with a local green and duck pond. As they arrived, Alexander opened the gates to a house that was so beautiful, Elizabeth just gasped. Sheila had heard all about the house, although she had never actually seen it. She could feel Elizabeth's excitement. Alexander explained that all the water and other utilities, such as the electric were switched on, so they could get a really good feel for the place.

Walking in through the huge oak door, they entered into a beautiful tiled hallway and an open staircase to the left hand side. There were rooms off to the right and to the left. There was a room at the end of the hall too. The smell of wood and fresh paint greeted them.

Some of the finishing touches had only recently been made, since the owner had decided to sell it through their business. The whole house seemed bathed in light. The staircase was split into an 'L' shape. The landing window was made in stained glass, with a beautiful lady dressed in a blue gown. She was surrounded by a pond with water lilies and held the most stunning bouquet of flowers in her hands. Her long hair was braided with flowers and ribbons. It truly was absolutely magnificent. Elizabeth had loved stained glass since she was a little girl. It had been one of the few pleasures of having to sit in church for hours.

Taking in the house, the attention to detail was incredible. Although a new build, it had been made to look like an original Victorian property. There were dado rails, ceiling roses and deep skirting boards in oak, which she adored. The doors too were panelled oak and had been lightly varnished. The handles and door furniture were gothic black. The light fittings were made of wrought iron and the chandelier overhanging the staircase, simply took her breath away. Each room had authentic-looking sash windows. They allowed light in everywhere, which she loved. It was spacious and she could easily visualise her furniture here, together with some new furnishings.

There were three reception rooms. Two had oak panelled flooring and the third with a lovely beige, deep pile carpet. Despite the fact that it was empty of furniture, she felt it was full of life and just ready for a family to move in straightaway. Elizabeth began shaking with excitement. She had thought one of the rooms could be used as a lounge, another a playroom and the remaining one a study or office. As she walked through the house, she knew this was to be her home. She thought the boys would be delighted too. She imagined their little faces when they wandered around here. The feeling of homeliness was becoming magnified, seemingly by the minute.

Upstairs there were four bedrooms and another in the attic space too. Absolutely perfect she thought, as the boys would have a room each. Besides her room, there were two spare bedrooms for visitors. There were Velux roof windows and reclaimed beams which had been restored to their original state. There was an en-suite bathroom in the Master bedroom, another along the main hallway upstairs and another in the attic room.

Being a detached property, she knew that noise would be at a minimum. What a relief, she thought. She looked through the upstairs windows at the rear garden. Though the plants were not yet established, she thought she would ask Sheila for her advice. There were fields and trees in the distance, so the boys would have plenty of space to play. She knew Ted would help too. Perhaps the boys would like a little den or a shed outside? There was also plenty of room for a Summer House. Looking down at the garden, she noticed there was an orangery too.

"Wow" she gasped. Sheila and Alexander loved it.

Though new to Sheila too, both women knew that this was a wonderful choice of home for Elizabeth and her family. They hugged one another on the landing before walking through to the bedrooms, one by one.

The attic room was absolutely stunning and Elizabeth decided that this would be her personal bedroom. Alexander wandered behind the two of them, conscious not to get in the way, though thrilled that they loved it so much. He had put so much effort and love into this place. If he had been in his younger years, he and his wife could have enjoyed it together with their young family. Thinking about his late, beloved wife, without either of the women noticing, he secretly and discreetly wiped silent tears from his eyes.

Returning downstairs they moved through to the dining kitchen. It was huge with an Aga and oak fitted units. The marble workshops and granite sink were perfect and in keeping with the rest of the house. There was also a utility room and wet room too. It was absolutely perfect. She felt so comfortable here, that she knew it would be the right place for her and her family to make up for all the lost time. Her heart seemed to leap inside her chest cavity. Sheila smiled at her as they sat for a moment at the huge dining table.

"The owner had this dining suite shipped over from Spain. I'm almost certain he had stated that he is happy to include it in the asking price if you do want it." He was finding it hard not to laugh now with excitement, as Sheila and Elizabeth were so happy and thrilled. They were just like two little girls together.

The orangery led off from the kitchen and was so full of light. Elizabeth wondered whether it would be nice to use this as a second dining room too. There were free standing Victorian radiators, so it obviously had heating facilities for those winter months. Elizabeth thought that this would be a perfect place to read and relax with the boys.

Sheila suggested they go out into the garden and the surrounding perimeters. They were more than happy with the decking, the patio area and especially the built in barbeque. Elizabeth found it so easy to visualise them all settled here and loved the thought of having quiet time to reflect in the garden. She had already decided to invite Alexander and Sheila for lunches and dinners. She knew she had bridges to build with Ted's sister Joanne and her children too. This was certainly the place to do it. *'To enjoy and to simply be' she thought.*

They ate the selection of cakes, as they sat on the garden bench overlooking the rear of the house. Elizabeth had Goosebumps throughout her whole body. Alexander was delighted that she loved it so much. Being an architect, this was certainly the most rewarding part of his work.

"I take it that your decision is made Elizabeth?" Looking across first at Sheila, then at Alexander, she nodded and let out a huge gasp of excitement.

"Yes, yes, yes."

"Well, the owner is happy for a quick sale. Most of the paperwork had already been carried out as it's a new build. I'm sure under the circumstances that since I know you and your family so well we could sort out a quick sale. How does within the month sound to you."

Chapter Twenty Six

Elizabeth was keen to get to know both Sheila and Alexander better. She wanted to build on the friendships and she certainly wanted to learn more about opening her heart centre and her soul. In many ways what she had experienced over the previous days had been overwhelming and she was aware that she had never reflected on her life before.

For the first time in her life, she was happy just to be and to just enjoy silence. This is what she needed now and she knew it. Despite missing the boys, she knew she needed time. Ted was happy to have the boys for a few more days, as she readjusted to her new life and her new outlook too. She had explained all that had happened in relation to the house sale and of course, Ted knew of the property anyway. He fully supported her in her decision. He agreed that it would be a wonderful home for them and said he would be happy to help with the move. He explained that it would be really easy to sell her apartment, they were highly sought after properties. He offered to help in any way possible.

Under the circumstances, Alexander had given her a set of keys for the house. Most of the paperwork had been completed and it was simply a matter of 'crossing the T's and dotting the I's'. He was happy to allow her to re-visit any time. She was free to move her furniture and possessions in there and begin to make it her home. She had asked Sheila about the garden and her ideas on its design. She knew she wanted colour and a mixture of evergreens, shrubs and plants that would spread, so that it would look like a real English cottage garden.

Since it was the school summer holidays, it was made so much easier because she could bring the boys with her. She certainly hadn't missed the school run. Her thoughts wandered back to all the people she had tried to impress previously, whilst dropping off and collecting her sons. Both she and Ted, were happy to find the boys a new school here in the country. Ted frequently travelled around the local villages and towns anyway with his work, so it would still be easy for him to see his sons.

Both he and Elizabeth were certainly getting along so much better now that she had opened her heart. They found it so much easier to discuss their son's future schools jointly. They were happy to view them together, once the school term re-started in September. Ted had kept in touch with her and simply stated;

"Just ask if you need anything."

Something seemed to shift inside her when she heard those words; *'Just ask.'* She had never found it easy to ask for help. She had certainly found it easy to *take* these last few years, though asking and receiving were becoming new experiences for her. She knew that as she was getting to know herself better, she needed time to herself.

She was glad that Ted had offered to have the boys for the extra few days, as it simply gave her *time.* She had time to organise the move and just to be. Her apartment held nothing for her anymore and apart from sleeping there, she decided that she would spend the bulk of her time elsewhere. Ted had put her in touch with a removals firm who would take care of absolutely everything. So, all in all, apart from getting rid of stuff which she did not want to take with her to her new home, there was very little to do at all. The time would give her time to reflect and start a new life with fulfilment.

Her apartment had sold within two days as expected and she had been offered the full asking price. They were cash buyers, so everything would be completed within the month, just as Alexander had suggested.

There seemed so much to do and yet she knew that she had so much support around her to make it simple. She recognised that her previous self would have made the house move into a complete drama. Now she just wanted peace and serenity. She was now allowing trust into her everyday life and was totally comfortable that all would be well.

Each day she visited the house and often just sat in the orangery, or the garden. She had purchased some furniture locally and was happy to just be. There seemed no need to rush and decide what was needed and for which room. *For now she simply wanted to just be.* Sitting here in this lovely space in a beautiful garden, she allowed her thoughts to drift. She was certainly missing her sons though spoke to them daily. She was grateful for Ted's understanding in so many ways. His words *'Just ask if you need anything'* kept repeating in her head. She thought about how rarely she had asked for help and recognised that she was now able to appreciate help.

How often had he offered and she had been dismissive! She remembered the evening when Sheila had asked her to stay over. She thought back to that morning when Alexander had assisted her too. She was finally both allowing and receiving, recognising this was to be a huge part of her life. She sat quietly each and every morning and checked in with Little Elizabeth, her younger self and would ask her what she wanted to do. Usually it was just to come here and watch the wildlife in the garden. Sometimes she requested a visit to the garden centre to see the huge variety of flowers and shrubs, not to mention the huge pond features with an accompanying aquarium where she would just love to look at the fish.

For the first time in her life, Elizabeth was experiencing *peace. Nothing had changed really apart from her! It had all been there previously. Her perception had changed, that was the key to the shift. She was now able to receive and see life differently. Her reflections were allowing her to embrace wisdom in to her daily life.*

She tried to think back to times when she had previously received so easily. Recollecting her life, there was nothing particularly, apart from the times when she was in absolutely desperate situations and she needed help. The one situation that came to mind immediately, was when she had gone into premature labour with their sons. Ted was away at their villa in France and seeing numerous clients whilst he was there. They had rowed before he left, so she had sat stewing and had been in tears, going over the repercussions of what had been said in the argument. He had said she 'was cold and isolating herself further and further away from him.' She remembered the deep, stabbing hurt when he had called her 'The Ice Maiden.'

Tears came easily at those memories and she could finally see what he had been trying to communicate to her. It had been so true at the time. She was terrified of being a mother, especially to twins. She was an only child and had no siblings to learn from. Having few friends also meant that her understanding of children and their needs was virtually non-existent. She was frightened, so very frightened, of getting it all wrong and being judged.

Her sister-in-law Joanne had two toddlers and seemed to be a perfect mother. Her boys were always well-behaved and good natured children. Her connection to Sheila was so wonderful, so that both mother and grandmother could share the joy of the children. She would often look on when she and Ted visited and she would feel so inadequate.

Joanne never seemed to sit still, she was often picking them up if they fell over in the garden, they got dirty, needed the toilet, or they needed their food cutting up at meal times. It was never ending. Joanne had eighteen months between her boys and was crazy busy. Elizabeth was about to get dropped in at the deep end with twins! Watching Joanne with Sheila, just made her more and more aware of the lack of the relationship with her and her mother. Besides that, Sheila had retired and Elizabeth's mother was still working full-time, not to mention all the other stuff she did throughout the week. She certainly didn't want to put the twins in a nursery, nor did she want a nanny. Ted's business was so successful, that he was getting busier week by week too.

She didn't feel that she could confide in Ted at the time, simply because she couldn't even formulate her actual feelings. They seemed to go from the joy of meeting her prospective sons, to absolute terror at the unknown. She now realised that fear had destroyed, or limited so many opportunities in her life.

The pregnancy itself had been really difficult. She started with incredible morning sickness, right from the early weeks and it just deteriorated from there. She would often try to vomit as soon as she would awaken in the morning and start to actually vomit, before even getting out of bed. The morning sickness soon became all day sickness and often she struggled to even keep a drink down. She had to be admitted to hospital on several occasions for treatment to rehydrate her in those early months.

All in all, the whole experience was already exhausting. She looked awful too, which for a woman who wanted nothing less than perfection, was a complete and utter disaster. The sickness had continued well into the second trimester. However, by this time she was at least willing to try Sheila's suggestions of ginger biscuits and arrowroot. As the twins grew in her belly, she loved to watch them kick and wondered whether one would be bigger than the other.

Carrying twins meant that she was regularly checked, especially with the earlier problems. They were assured that both babies were growing well, though she had been warned that she might need a caesarean section, if one of the boys was breech. Added to the mix, she wondered how she would cope with having surgery too. Her fears were certainly running away with her, though she could find no way of slowing them down. Sheila had purchased some meditation CDs for her, which further enforced her thoughts that she was a "witch bitch.'

"If only" she said out loud, without even realising that she had uttered anything. She surprised herself by her words and when she looked at the time, decided to make herself something to eat. Alexander had given her free range to use the house and the facilities. She had purchased several items for the kitchen already, a toaster, kettle and some cutlery and crockery too. She had found some great pans and baking utensils in the local supermarket and was pleased that it was all coming together.

As she settled down enjoying her stir fry, she looked around the kitchen and felt as though the whole house was wrapping itself around her like a protective bubble. How wonderful she thought, as she wondered how the boys would react to being here.

Chapter Twenty Seven

Returning home to her apartment that evening was becoming more and more difficult by the day now. She started to run the bath and used the Epsom salts as Sheila had suggested. Sheila had mentioned that they would keep her energies clean, whilst she managed her transition. She felt the connection to Sheila daily, even though she hadn't seen her for a few days. She wondered whether she was thinking of her too and was she sending healing? She certainly felt a warmth and a comfort too.

The bath had become her sanctuary now as she made time to just be. For the first time in her life she was actually looking forward to each and every day and *allowing what was to come, rather than forcing each and every aspect.* She was wondering why she had wanted so much control for so long. Learning now to rest and relax meant that she also realised just how exhausting her previous lifestyle had been.

Her thoughts drifted to her own parents, as she remembered just how little quality time she had spent with them. Soon after Elizabeth was born her mother had attended law school and trained as a lawyer. She was often studying in the evenings and at the weekends too, so they had very little time together. Her father too was a busy man, working for the police as an undercover officer. His shifts were so changeable and he too was often too tired to play with her.

Her maternal grandparents looked after her most of the time, whilst her parents were working or studying. They were too old and grumpy to be bothered and, as she thought back to those times, she re-remembered how she would only get attention if she was well-behaved and quiet. She had once danced and jumped on the bed upstairs and been so severely scolded. She was subsequently made to sit facing the wall for the rest of the day, with only water at various intervals.

Laughter and fun, precious childhood memories had evaded her and her only limited pleasure came when they attended Sunday mass at the local church. She would always be dressed smartly and had to sit properly and not fidget. As time went on and her mother gained her qualifications, she would buy lots of presents for Elizabeth; which she was now realising were merely compensation for her lack of *time and attention*. Guilt was something which had become familiar to Elizabeth as a youngster, when she had *apparently misbehaved*. Now guilt dominated her thoughts again, as she was beginning to comprehend her lack of maternal skills with her treasured twin sons, Will and Ben.

Growing up as an only child she was only ever recognised when she did well in her exams, gaining high academic results had been her only aim. Luckily academic study was easy to her, as reading was a quiet occupation that she was allowed to do whilst with her grandparents. Her parents were so well known in the local community that she always knew the pressure was on for her to be well-dressed, well-mannered and tidy.

Her childhood memories passed by, as she recalled the envy she felt at the other children, who told her their stories of picnics in the park with their families and adventures of climbing trees and exploring the countryside. She envied their stories of imaginary pirates & monsters played out under bed sheets, in cupboards and wardrobes. They told her about hide and seek, as she had never actually played it before and exactly what the rules of the game were.

She pondered now just how different life would be and how different it would have been, had she had a more nurtured beginning. She loved her parents and her grandparents, though wondered what each of their inner child would think. Having twins meant that she had their toys and games in the apartment, even though they were always tidied away out of sight.

She decided that she would look through them after her bath and ask Little Elizabeth just what she wanted to do. Once she had towelled herself down she led quietly on the bed for a few minutes before getting dressed simply in to her nightshirt. Inner Elizabeth was wide awake and excited as she wandered into her son's room. She had always loved to colour when she was younger and she was grateful that her sons had several colouring books. She knew they would be only too pleased to know that she had borrowed them. She looked through the games too and found Jenga.

It was two hours later, when she was disturbed by the phone. As she answered, she could see on the screen that it was Ted.

"Hello" Elizabeth answered.

"Hello it's Ted, the boys are in bed, they've had had a wonderful day at the beach and they are missing you."

She knew he was delighted and surprised too. She chatted easily and was relieved that the mask, which she had previously worn when in communication with him, was definitely non-existent. Ted continued;

"I'm more than willing to have them for another couple of days, though I'm merely suggesting that maybe we meet up tomorrow? Maybe we could both take the boys to the new house together? Otherwise, I've already spoken to mum and she is happy for us all to meet up there, at her place?"

Elizabeth had certainly missed the boys and had been grateful for his help. She was quite excited at the thought of seeing them and was also surprised, that she was also looking forward to seeing Ted too.

"Leave it with me and I will either call, or text you in the morning. Yes, it sounds like a plan either way. It would be so lovely to see them both. Do you have a preference?"

"No" said Ted.

"Ok I'll listen to my intuition and call you back. Thank you for your thoughtfulness Ted. Speak later."

Putting the phone down, she returned to the childhood colouring and playing. She had found some bubbles to blow and opened the balcony windows to enable her to watch the bubbles fly, wherever they desired. She made a decision to blow bubbles more often, to laugh and to smile at each and every opportunity.

Chapter Twenty Eight

What a superb project her new home would be! She and Ted had agreed that they would keep the new home a secret until Elizabeth felt ready to show them around. Today was definitely the day. She was excited and they had agreed to meet after lunch. Sheila had been asked to meet them there, along with Alexander, as both she and Ted felt that seeing the joy and surprise of their sons would be something to be celebrated. They were all invited for an evening meal at Sheila's later that afternoon.

Elizabeth was pleased the arrangements had been made the previous evening as when she woke up she felt excited and thrilled. Being an interior designer herself, she remembered decorating a house very similar to this many years ago. In the previous few days, Elizabeth had decided that she would once again take up her interior design business. The whole experience had made her realise that she had forgotten just how much it had meant to her. She missed the buzz it had always given her and the thrill of making a house a home. Something which sadly she had forgotten to do in her own home. That's how she and Ted had met all those years ago at an 'Ideal Home' exhibition. The memories and many others brought a huge smile to her face. They were so in love with one another back then. They shared so much joy and laughter together. They would discuss building projects for their mutual clients and really bounced ideas off each other so easily.

His business was by far so much more successful and over the years she had begun to feel more and more inadequate. He reminded her constantly that he was building the homes and business properties for very wealthy professionals. There was bound to be more money in that, than in her line of work. His reassurance that he loved her for her, not for her business, nor her success. He was simply happy to be with her regardless. Her insecurities began to get the better of her and over the years they became stronger and ever more destructive as the months and years passed by.

More and more, she was trying too hard to impress clients, whilst watching his business just grow and grow. She realised with great sadness now that she had been so jealous. Her painful memories reminded her just how difficult it must have been for Ted, to just watch her insecurities destroy what had once been a great friendship and a once wonderful marriage.

The twins hadn't been planned. She had been on the contraceptive pill and had had a sickness bug. She was so surprised at the news, whereas Ted's delight was overflowing. She was so angry when she found out that he had told his family and friends, work colleagues and anyone who would listen about their news. She was simply still trying to get her head around it! Looking back she really was such a grouch! 'Poor Ted', she thought. She felt that she had spoilt so much of his joy over the years.

By wanting to please everyone else and him too, she had lost herself and despite his constant encouragement for her to continue her business, she had eventually just let it dwindle. Now she realised the impact, that the resentment that this had had on their marriage, not to mention the other stresses, premature twins and his father's illness.

Chapter Twenty Nine

Today was a new beginning. She was beginning to forgive herself on a deeper level daily now. As she recalled their conversation at Sheila's house the other night, where he had patiently explained so much about esoteric wisdom, it was now quite clear that he had already done the bulk of his forgiveness for her actions already. His manner had been full of loving kindness and there were certainly no undercurrents of anger and hurt.

Now she was learning to forgive herself. She knew a new and even better version of Elizabeth was unfolding. She was definitely feeling that by moving to their new home, the forgiveness process would be greatly assisted. Her new self was in the making. The new house was definitely part of the bigger picture and she knew that the house and the surrounding garden would be where she would grow and be nurtured. She had definitely outgrown her apartment. Today was certainly that new beginning.

The twins hadn't been told where they were going that day and didn't think it unusual that Alexander should be with them. He often accompanied them on so many of their days out. He was a part of the family after all these years. They knew they were all sharing a meal together at Grandma's later and they would be staying with mum again.

She was looking forwards to meeting them all at 2pm, in what was soon to be their new home. She was aware whilst driving there, that the house needed a name too. Maybe they could discuss that over dinner this evening? Just what should she call her new home and her new venture?

She arrived earlier than she had expected, as the traffic was lighter than she had thought. Maybe it was also that many people were on holiday, she mused. She had over twenty minutes before everyone else was due, so had a quick look around and then wandered around the garden.

Both she and Ted were happy to see just how the boys reacted. They had agreed to discuss the décor for their individual bedrooms as per their wishes. Now they were able to put aside their differences, or rather she was, they were happy to purchase their bedroom furniture together. The boys were so aware of the change in their mother and obviously thrilled, though they had no idea about this place. What a wonderful surprise it would be. Neither did they know that they would have their own playroom and a guest bedroom for their friends and cousins too.

Wandering around her new home, she was so thrilled to be able to finally share it with her sons. She hadn't seen them in the last few days and was really looking forward to spending time with them. The arrangements had already been made that they would all be having a meal at Sheila's later.

She looked at the young trees that had been recently planted and visualised what they might look like fully grown. She had decided that a tree house and den for the boys would mean that they had their own space, especially now that they were almost in double figures. She was happy to let Ted sort out 'The Man Cave' for them. She had a knowing that Alexander would love to be involved too and was happy to encourage his opinions, knowing that they would all agree anyway.

It wasn't long before the doorbell rang. There they were, her beautiful sons, her ex-husband, Sheila and Alexander. Of course, the boys had known Alexander for years. They were all so at ease with one another. Elizabeth was still getting used to being at ease. She was so glad that she was a quick learner! The boys rushed to her and grabbed her waist. Evidently thrilled to see her, they each took one of her hands as everyone wandered into the house.

They were obviously very happy with the place and within a few minutes after they had arrived, they just happily ventured off and began to look around.

Elizabeth hadn't really expected them to be so at ease in a new place and she wasn't quite sure how to handle the situation. Watching her and knowing how much it meant to all the adults to share this experience, Ted gently called them.

"Cor blimey, we really like this place dad, it's got real taste and it feels really nice too. It's massive like Grandma's house and we can play football in the hallway. The stained glass window is really fabulous too. Are you selling it to one of your clients Dad? Do you like it Grandma? What do you think Great Uncle Alex?" They were clearly delighted.

Elizabeth was very close to tears and she was grateful Sheila stepped in quickly to save the day:

"This is a very special project boys, Uncle Alexander designed it. We would all like your opinion, so, if it's okay with you two, we would like you to walk around the house and give us your honest thoughts about the rooms, the design and whatever else you think. Where would you like to start?"

Elizabeth breathed out a very deep sigh of relief and thanked Sheila without the need for words.

"So you designed this Great Uncle Alexander. It's really amazing. Let's start in the kitchen then." Being twins the boys would often talk in unison with one another.

They all pottered into the kitchen and as Alexander had designed the house, they all gestured that he should lead them from room to room, after they had looked around the kitchen. They loved it. Pure and simple. They just loved it. The boys had often heard their father and Alexander chatting about various house designs. They were quite at ease discussing window sizes and shapes, differing staircases and building materials too. Here was a wide variety of building materials, designs and although a new build, they were evidently impressed that it was in keeping with an old Victorian home.

"These rooms are massive, I love the flooring and the huge windows too." Ben was definitely taken with the place.

"I love the high ceilings and the woodwork dad, I think Great Uncle Happy Harry has helped too?" Will's delight was evident.

They all burst out laughing. As they moved from room to room, they viewed the garden from the landing and from each of the upstairs bedroom windows, they were clearly thrilled. The huge stained glass window was such an amazing feature too. Everyone admired that. The attic room was definitely a huge winner and the orangery too. Looking at one another, Will announced on behalf of both of them

“Yes, we love it. Great Uncle Alexander, you are the greatest. Well done. So when are you selling it then?”

Ted and Sheila looked across at Elizabeth and although the boys had their eyes on Alexander, when he also looked across at Elizabeth, the secret was out.

“Mum, you’re buying it!” Will jumped for joy first, whilst Ben was still joining the dots. Seconds later Ben burst out laughing.

“Can we choose our bedrooms Mummy, please? Right now. Please?”

Both of them obviously thought the attic room was cool and were disappointed to learn that it was already taken for Mum.

“Ahhhhhh no, oh well, let’s go back upstairs then and choose.” Off they rushed, it wasn’t long before they had made up their minds, although they were reassured that as the house had five bedrooms, they could change rooms if they so desired.

Elizabeth said that she had brought some cakes to celebrate and suggested they all have a drink in the orangery. The boys were given free range to go wherever they wanted. They ran around the house again and soon returned asking a variety of questions.

“Why has it got five bedrooms, when there are only three of us and we have shared a room at your old apartment? Why are there so many bathrooms? Can we have a tree house? Can Great Uncle Alexander build us a den?”

Elizabeth explained that the extra bedrooms were for visitors and their other cousins too. She explained that with three reception rooms, they could also have a playroom too. The twins were so delighted to hear that news. Never had they had ever been allowed visitors at the apartment before.

"We really love it Mum. When can we move in?

By now they were jumping up and down. They kept running around the house and the adults just left them to it and retired into the garden. The adults all smiled and as each one looked towards the others, they all knew this was definitely the right decision and the right time too.

Before leaving, they all took one last look around. Alexander was so proud of his workmanship. Elizabeth explained that she felt the house needed a name and she asked if it was alright to discuss that over dinner at Sheila's. As she locked the door she said a quiet prayer that they would be settled here within the next fortnight or so. She too was filled with joy and excitement. Although new feelings to her, she was loving them and feeling more grateful as life began to unfold.

Chapter Thirty

Arriving at Sheila's they all gathered in the garden, just as they usually did. It was a lovely hot summer day. After having some cordial, the boys went off to their den. Sheila had bought some very expensive champagne and offered a toast. She said they were all welcome to stay the night and the food would be ready within the hour. Conversation was easy and Elizabeth was keen to get to know Alexander and Sheila better too. Ted sat beside her and kept a watchful eye on the boys. Alexander was loving spending time with them and the men folk eventually disappeared after a while to find Will and Ben.

Elizabeth and Sheila began laying the huge patio table outside and the boys appeared requesting yet another drink.

"It's really hot out there Mummy. We love our new house and we are trying to think of a name. Daddy and Great Uncle Alexander are being really silly, saying it should be called 'The Bat Cave', 'The Boys Den' or 'Alexander Palace, Footy Mansion' and lots of other silly things. They keep laughing at their own jokes. We've come to help you with dinner to get away from them!"

Sheila and Elizabeth were in stitches at the ridiculous names.

"Come and help us lay the table for dinner then boys." With those words they were off, back into the den.

Dinner was served, melon to start with prawn cocktail. Then salad and a huge variety of cooked meats and different breads too. Alexander loved Greek food so there were olives, feta, zucchini fritters and dolmades. They all felt very hungry. Elizabeth delighted in the simplicity of them all being here sharing a meal. Ben sat right next to her and kept stroking her hair and looking at her.

"I really missed you Mummy." Will looked over at his mother and smiled.

They were all aware of how much the simplicity of eating outdoors, enjoying good food, great company and superb conversation meant to them. The food was so tasty and it was so wonderful to eat at a slow pace. Alexander really loved eating and chatting without the need to rush. It had always been part of his much loved culture. Being a widower he valued his extended family very much. He watched them all interacting and inevitably, as he always did, he thought back to his late wife and William too. Often he would imagine them watching down from Heaven with the Gods and smiling.

Fruit salad and baklava were served before the coffees. They were all loving the whole experience. Sheila loved cooking and preparing food for her guests. Having her family around was always a delight.

She felt there was a certain magic in the air today. Once again she watched closely over her beloved son Ted. She was aware that he was still very much in love with Elizabeth and always had been. 'Patience and time' she thought, 'patience and time.' It had been hard for her when they divorced, as she wondered just how much contact Elizabeth would allow him. Despite knowing that at the time Elizabeth was happy to allow anyone to have them, she really wanted her grandsons to grow up with their father in their lives and to know their roots.

Sheila felt so happy that so much had now changed and watching Elizabeth blossom into her true self. “Mummy please can we have a fish pond with some Koi carp?” Will asked.

Elizabeth looked over at Ted and wondered what his thoughts were.

“Leave it with me boys and I’ll discuss it with your father, Alexander and Grandma. How’s that?”

After the meal the weather was still beautiful and the temperature about twenty degrees. Sheila had made some sassy water with garden mint, grated fresh ginger, sliced cucumber and slices of lemon. Her close friend Molly had made her some years ago whilst they were at college together. They were all grateful for the welcome refreshment it offered.

Everyone was happy just to be after the meal and they sat watching the leaves move with the gentle breezes. From time to time the boys went off into the den or to watch the fish in the pond. They always loved feeding them at this time of the evening.

“Come and help us mummy” they requested.

Elizabeth could not resist her sons request and off they went to the pond. She had never really paid much attention to the pond and the fish before. The water lilies were so beautiful creating much needed shade for the fish. They were quite used to being fed at this time and certainly used to the boys as they threw the fish sticks into the water. Being aware of her inner child now she felt Little Elizabeth was thoroughly enjoying the experience. She was so delighted. Elizabeth agreed they could have a pond and it would be quite a good size too. The garden at the new house was certainly large enough and Alexander had said that if she did ever want more land, the adjoining field was available. Sheila's pond was fitted with a beautiful fountain and Elizabeth knew that she had someone to maintain it for her every few months. The decision was made.

Returning to the house, the boys wanted to play cricket. Ted and Alexander joined in whilst Elizabeth and Sheila chatted easily. The time was by now getting up towards nine.

"Come on boys, time for bath and bed." They were shattered and without any arguments they returned from the garden whilst their bath was run for them. Ted was happy to bathe them as the women chatted with Alexander. Once bathed and in their pyjamas, the twins came to say 'goodnight' whilst Ted waited upstairs for them to return so that he could read them a story.

Elizabeth asked for more details as to how Sheila and Alexander had met. Sheila said she would gather some photographs. She returned with a leather-bound photograph album and by the time Ted appeared, they were laughing at the old fashioned clothing and various hair styles which Sheila had had over the years. There was an evident sadness looking through photographs of the loss of William and Alexander's late wife too. A sobering thought that life was precious and fragile.

Despite being invited to stay, Alex and Ted both expressed their gratitude and also their apologies as they declined Sheila's incredibly kind offer. Both men were wise enough to know that the women needed time to continue to get to know one another. With the boys asleep in bed, now was a perfect opportunity. Hugs and kisses were passed around as the men shared a taxi to their separate homes.

Chapter Thirty One

The two women were really pleased to be spending time together. Elizabeth wanted to understand Sheila more and knew that this would in turn assist her in helping her to understand herself. She had heard other people call it *'being asleep or disconnected.'* Sheila had often mentioned it when they had chatted and she had explained about the heart centre opening. Elizabeth was beginning to wish that she had wakened up earlier.

Looking through the photographs was a great way to start the conversation.

"Please tell me more about your life Sheila, it would help me to understand you more."

Sheila was wise enough to know that Elizabeth wanted to get to know her more, so that she could understand how Sheila became so spiritually aware.

"Goodness, well I guess we have all night then, since the boys are in bed. It's quite a story and I hope it helps you with your soul journey too. I grew up in London, with my four older brothers. My parents had strong morality and enforced strict rules and decency into us all.

As the youngest, with four older brothers, I was inevitably a bit of a 'Tomboy.' I was always happy to climb trees and play football, doing the rough and tumble seemed normal to me. Mum used to make us all help in the kitchen, even the boys so there seemed no difference between the masculine and feminine in that department. We lived in a tiny back to back, terraced house in London near the dockland. As a youngster I had a best friend called Michael. I truly don't recall how long we had been friends. His mother and mine were best friends, so I guess that we probably exchanged glances from our prams." Sheila was obviously happy to continue:

"Mum and Fanny had been great friends and when she had lost her husband, their friendship deepened as Fanny needed support to raise a growing family. I recall Fanny and her family staying with us, making the house even more cramped. No-one bothered though as we just truly loved having them around. We were youngsters and we used to get up to all sorts of mischief. We never did anything bad as such, just kid-stuff." Elizabeth happily listened to Sheila's story, though became aware that the tone of Sheila's voice was changing.

"One particular day we climbed the rigging of an old disused cruiser. We had done it hundreds of times before. Michael climbed up and just seemed to lose his footing, when a huge siren and the noise of the seagulls caught him off guard." Sheila paused as she recalled that sound. Elizabeth waited patiently for her to continue.

"Watching his body fall was one of the most painful moments of my life to be honest, besides losing William. It was such a horrid thud. It was surreal in many ways and I waited for him to talk or shout to me. I knew he was dead when I 'saw a lighter version of him' very much like Patrick Swayze's character in the film 'Ghost.' Do you recall the scene when he passes into the light, towards the end of the film? I'd had a bad feeling all day. I was too young and inexperienced to know what it meant at the time." Sheila sighed before continuing:

"I was mute for quite a while after that. The doctors said it was shock and trauma. I didn't return to the local school after that fateful day. Unless I was with another family member I didn't go out, neither would mother allow me out. I later found out that the Bradley's had threatened the whole family, especially me. One thing I certainly do recall was my mother's sobs on the day of his funeral. Obviously, unbeknown to me at the time, we had been warned not to attend." She breathed out another huge sigh.

"Often these things, even though they are awful, turn out for the best. My father's extended family had settled in Kent and we had visited frequently over the previous years. Knowing our circumstances, the local land owner had been approached by my father's cousin Bob, to ask if we as a family, could be assured work and a place to live. Mr Marsh welcomed us with open arms within weeks.

During the time when I was mute, my intuition became stronger by the day. I would know things before they would happen and I became really in tune with animals too. I felt Michael around most days and my artwork became more detailed and prestigious. My hearing was greatly sharpened too." Sheila paused to ensure Elizabeth was listening to her story.

"The day we moved we were all so excited to be honest. My brother Harry and I had always been close though after the accident he rarely left my side. We were huddled together on the cart when we arrived at our beautiful cottage in the countryside. We all loved it and we all settled in really quickly. My eldest two brothers worked the land with dad. Mum got a job in the manor house. She thrived and although I sometimes caught her crying; as I knew she still missed Michael and Fanny, I know she was the happiest she had ever been."

From her description it was clear to Elizabeth that Sheila obviously loved the country life. She smiled as she continued:

"It wasn't long before we were invited to the manor house and Mr and Mrs Marsh delighted in showing me a room with so much artwork, that I thought I had died and gone to heaven. The couple really encouraged me in my drawings, sketching and painting. They also paid for me to have a private tutor to educate me, as I had missed so much school. Harry and I really loved the tutor as he would often sit in on my Maths lesson or English too. Miss Black, my tutor was a spinster and a very gifted teacher. I knew intuitively that she had had a really tough upbringing and she was glad of employment away from her hometown and family. I still hear from her occasionally. Maybe I should write to her?" Sheila paused whilst she thought of her old teacher.

"Anyways, I progressed very quickly and soon made up for the time I had lost. Mr and Mrs Marsh showed us nothing but kindness. There was no hidden agenda. It was just plain and simple that they seemed to get so much pleasure from seeing the whole family thrive. It seems too simple though that's the absolute beauty of it. It was simple. We all lived in a beautiful part of the world and the community was a very strengthening one. We were all wise enough to know that by helping each other, we actually helped ourselves. I guess once again that we are back to the law of attraction.

Life was great and being away from the city meant that I had endless things to sketch and inspire me. I loved the architecture and Harry and I would just sit and be. He would often carve a bird, or a leaf from either wood or stone. I would sketch too. We were truly blessed after the horrors of Michael's death. I still think of him and sometimes I still feel him around, even after all these years." Sheila paused to sip her drink.

"One day I showed Mr Marsh some of Harrys works as I was taking them in a basket up to the house. I intended to paint or sketch them. He was very impressed. He saw Harry's talent and simply wanted to encourage him to reach his full potential. A few months later he arranged for Harry to work in France on some restoration projects. Later that year, he was off to France to become an apprentice stonemason and carpenter. He loved it and would return as often as he could. Inevitably life moved on and although I missed him, I too was flowering." Sheila's eyes sparkled and it was so clear that she loved her brother Harry.

"Mr Marsh had spoken often with my tutor about my progress. She had suggested I attend architectural college. Her eye for detail in my drawings and sketches was amazing. I found out later that her father had been a very famous architect. My parents were asked about their opinions and I was certainly ready to move on. Since Harry had moved away I knew my turn would soon come. It felt so right. I remember getting Goosebumps all over me, when I was asked if I wanted to do architecture as a career." Sheila smiled as she continued:

"I had always loved the old buildings in London. Those in Kent were really amazing and I truly loved to sketch. It felt perfect so, all in all, the jigsaw pieces just slipped into place easily. That's where I met William of course and I guess you know the story of how we met? Very soon after our initial meeting we were married. It was indeed love at first sight and we were lucky enough to be given a cottage near my parents as the college wasn't too far away." Sheila's love for her late husband was clear as she cleared her throat and wiped away a tear before continuing:

"We knew we would love our work and even when we had to study it never seemed a chore. Getting stuck in on various projects and building sites was also easy and so enjoyable to us both. Within a year or two we met Alexander and he was such a lost soul. His English was so broken and he obviously missed his home country and the culture. The weather here was really getting him down too. We happily helped him improve his language skills and we learnt so much from him too. We loved listening to his accent and loved our time together. He was an exceptionally talented man and despite the language barrier, we learnt so much from him. His family were very wealthy and had a massive construction company throughout Greece." Elizabeth was thrilled to learn so much from Sheila.

"We used to have so much fun together and my family loved him dearly. He quickly learnt the language though I'm not sure even now, whether he really finds it easy to cope with our weather! I would often leave them alone together; William and Alexander, they were like brothers in so many ways. I liked to have time alone with my mother, Clara, or to visit The Marshes. When Harry returned the following summer and met Alexander they hit it off immediately. Alexander was thrilled to find that Harry spoke almost fluent Greek." Elizabeth excused herself to the bathroom before Sheila began again.

"The Marshes were very well organised and forward- thinking business folk. They helped us set up our business in return for a small percentage of the profits. As you know the three of us started out together. I specialised in old architecture and William in the new. Alexander could turn his hand to anything and of course was aware of the Venetian architecture, not to mention the Greek, Roman and Italian. He and his family had travelled extensively so together we were quite a team, especially with the financial support and Mr Marshes business contacts. The fact that we all got along was a miracle too."

Sheila's attitude and demeanour changed suddenly and Elizabeth just waited for her to continue.

"Our marriage was wonderful for many years. We were very established in our field when Ted and Joanne arrived into the world. I was happy to give up work completely, as he kept me informed and often took me to projects they were building, or restoration work that they were undertaking. Ted grew up with it all and it's hardly surprising that he followed in our footsteps. Joanne was a beautiful dancer so we naturally encouraged her to dance. As you know she has her own very successful dance school now." Sheila's eyes began to water and her breathing changed as she explained:

"William was very ill with suspected meningitis when Ted was ten years old. He was rushed to the local hospital after he had collapsed suddenly. It was touch and go for several days. He was unconscious for that time. My parents helped out with the children, so I could visit and the thought of losing him became so uppermost in my thoughts. Our life had been wonderful and we really did have a perfect marriage."

Elizabeth could see, hear and feel Sheila's emotional pain as she recollected the memories.

"It was months before he was able to return to work, even part time. The doctors said that often an illness like this could cause mood swings and symptoms of anxiety. To be honest I ignored their warnings and stayed as positive as I could. Ted and Joanne were thriving at school and with the support from my family, Alexander and his wife too, we managed. The business was expanding rapidly and with William out of action, I returned to work part-time, whilst he had much needed time to convalesce." Elizabeth felt the weight of the emotion in the room and also felt tears in her eyes.

"We employed a male nurse to come and stay with us throughout that time and he took care of William very well. We had moved into the original part of this house and had just started renovation work and the extension, when William took ill. Everything was on hold and the whole house covered in dust and the usual clutter that any building site has to offer! We had bathroom suites, a huge variety of tiles, a kitchen sink, a wide variety of flat packed furniture and some new fitted kitchen units all over the place. Alexander suggested putting a caravan in the garden as we also had to accommodate our guests too, not to mention the nurse." Sheila was delighted to see that Elizabeth was enjoying learning about her life.

"It was very challenging to be honest. William was so poorly, so weak and virtually helpless. My family were tired coming backwards and forwards from Kent. Harry was away, although he said he would be happy to come and help. I tried my best to keep a brave face, especially in front of the children. They had no idea that their father had almost died. All our savings were tied up in renovating our home and with the business losing money, it just all got on top of me one day. William was still poorly and when he saw me crying, he thought that I didn't love him anymore which was so far from the truth. We hadn't made love for months by this point and the doctors had advised him to sleep alone, so he could recover more quickly." She dried her tears before carrying on with her story.

"Once he did recover, it took another eighteen months to rebuild the business back to its original glory as it was. The construction work on the house could begin again, though the project didn't appeal to me as much as it had done when we had made the original plans, almost two years earlier. I was exhausted, mentally, physically, emotionally and spiritually. I felt like I'd been through a masher. Over the coming months I was so thrilled to have my husband back on form." Sheila paused:

"Inevitably, I got pregnant within a few months. I knew I was carrying twins well before I had the scan. As I said earlier, my intuition had been very prominent since Michael's death. I knew something was very wrong. He was thrilled when he found out we were expecting and it seemed to help him get even stronger. The house was still only part finished and although Harry had returned and was a huge help, the business was expanding so rapidly that we simply couldn't keep up with everything.

Maybe it was because I was pregnant that my sensitivity was heightened. The scan revealed twins as I had expected. William was thrilled. The nagging feeling that something was wrong just seemed to get stronger daily. I truly do not know exactly when it was, but I asked the doctors to double check the twins. I was due to have a second scan the following morning. In the early hours of that horrid, horrid day, I was rushed to hospital with severe haemorrhaging. William had to make the decision whilst I was under anaesthetic to either save my life, or that of the twins. At only twenty six weeks pregnancy they would not be likely to survive. William stated later that one twin was dead on delivery and the other survived for two hours only. When I regained consciousness I was devastated and cried for several days. He just didn't know how to handle the situation at all. After all the bliss we had had and all we had shared, this seemed so unfair.

Recovering from surgery and suffering from a broken heart was difficult and challenging. Even when we know intuitively that things are not quite right, being human means that we feel the pain. Having to explain the loss to Ted and Joanne was awful. They had been so excited for things to work out and to be able to spoil their new siblings. I cried for several weeks after that. I think it was all the collective trauma of losing Michael, then Harry's leaving, William's illness and then the loss of the twins. Not to mention the house being topsy-turvy for well over a year." Sheila was crying now.

"Eventually things settled down, we employed more staff and set up our own training school for upcoming apprentices. Once the house was finished, I returned to work part-time and life carried on. William and I were as close as ever. However on rare occasions, he would become terrified that I would leave him for another man; the doctor had said it may have been as a result of his illness. I was never sure to be honest. It was difficult to reason with him and I have to admit that at times I felt challenged, though I just knew that eventually he would return to his normal self." Sheila sighed as she reminisced.

"Our industry is obviously predominantly male, although I have never even looked at another man in that way. William was always my true soul companion, my best friend, father to my children and as such, he could never be replaced. It was such a horrid situation when he doubted me and my trust, it was so very upsetting and to be honest, incredibly draining at times. Having to constantly reassure him, that I loved him dearly and couldn't even comprehend ever leaving his side."

Elizabeth saw the distress in Sheila's eyes and felt it in her heart too. Having been so self-absorbed for so many years, she had remained completely unaware of this woman's pain. Sheila's endurance, love, patience, integrity and character certainly shone. She was touched and thrilled that Sheila could now be honest and open with her. They had a break whilst they both enjoyed a hot chocolate and reflected on the day.

"We still haven't named your house." Sheila said.

"Though I'm sure it'll not take too much longer."

Pondering upon her new home for a few moments, Elizabeth thought back to the times, up until recently she had mostly found her boys to be a chore, listening to Sheila's evident pain at the loss of her own unborn twins touched her heart. How sad it was that she had been ignorant to all these things until now and she felt she had wasted so much time.

Distracting herself from her thoughts, she looked up at the side table where Sheila kept her latest read. She usually had a book, or three, on the go at once that she loved to devour. Sheila noticed her admiring the books.

"Oh, this one is a firm favourite. It's by Goldie Hawn, you know the actress. She was, well still is, Joanne's idol. It's simply called 'Goldie.' She is a very talented lady and it's her autobiography. That woman is a diamond. I'm thoroughly loving it and Joanne has leant it to me, though you're very welcome to borrow it after I have finished it. If you would like to?" Sheila passed the book to her and read the full title:

"Goldie; A Lotus Grows In The Mud."

What a wonderful book cover. She was certainly impressed. They had almost finished their drinks now and as Elizabeth stood up to pass the book back to Sheila, she started laughing:

"Golden Lotus House' what do you think?" Elizabeth suggested, her excitement clear from her tone of voice and the huge smile that seemed to stretch from ear to ear.

"I really love the name. The boys have asked for a pond in the garden and we talked about water lilies earlier? The Buddhists always use the lotus as a symbol of enlightenment. Wow. It was there all the time. I spotted that book the other day and should have listened to my intuition more carefully. The lotus grows from the mud, just as I have grown from the treacle, or the mud of life's ups and downs."

She was now experiencing Goosebumps all over her body and as Sheila nodded her agreement, they both arose to hug each other.

They cleared the cups away and then Sheila continued with her story.

"Once things had settled again Harry very kindly offered to take the whole family to Barcelona, in Spain. As a treat he had organised for us to have a private tour of the famous Sagrada Familia. He knew many of the architects on the project and had worked there briefly himself too. We were allowed into the beautiful cathedral an hour before the masses of tourists would descend. The attention to detail was jaw dropping. The magnificent stained-glass windows were absolutely stunning, as the morning light filtered in to the sacred space. The quality of workmanship was truly astounding. We were shown around by a local man who had worked on the place for many years. His knowledge about the original architect and its history left us completely astounded at the determination and courage needed to finish this building. Joanne and Ted absolutely loved everything about it. They walked around hand in hand with their favourite uncle.

We were in awe of the incredible ceilings and just how amazing one man's vision could be. The guide explained that millions of visitors passed through this place annually. As a very spiritually aware group of people, we could quite easily feel its' power. The amount of love that swept right through the whole place was truly touching. Sacred geometry was to be seen everywhere and we knew that all who would visit would, to one degree or another, be upgraded and enhanced spiritually."

She was very animated as she described the crypt and the outer walls too. Elizabeth thought back to the time that Ted had asked her if she would like to visit there for their honeymoon. She had declined thinking it was too common and was more concerned about impressing her friends at the time. Maybe it would have opened her heart centre earlier she thought. Reading her thoughts, Sheila continued to explain:

"The Black Madonna in the crypt had so much powerful energy. To be honest when I looked up at the statue, I felt quite dizzy and luckily William was holding my hand anyway. I had to sit down for several minutes, whilst the children wandered off with Harry.

Harry was so kind and whilst working there, one of the men had also told him about Monserrat. He knew I loved singing and music. All those years ago he had taken his friends' advice and visited there himself. Knowing that we would love it too, he had booked us a hotel there for the following day so that we could visit the Black Madonna and listen to the famous boys' choir. They are very precious memories now. I have the photographs somewhere you know. I'm sure the twins would love to visit. I seem to recall Ted saying that he would take them now they are old enough to appreciate it."

The women smiled a knowing smile that indeed they would visit these sacred places. The story continued:

"Harry was loving it all too. It was rare for us to have so much time together away from work. He truly loved the children and was very close to both of them. He paid for our fabulous luxury hotel and we all thoroughly enjoyed a tour of the city. You know Elizabeth, I have so many precious memories and I count my blessings daily. I think of Michael often and from time to time I feel his presence too. I am blessed that I have had a beautiful family and had the honour of bringing up my own two beauties. I have met some wonderful people along the way and worked in some of the most amazing places in the world." Sheila paused and smiled.

"I have a choice to feel my sadness as each day passes that I lost my one, true love, or I have a choice to trust that he watches over us from above and that we are not separated at all. William's demise was so dreadfully sad to me. It broke my heart to think that he wouldn't get to see his beloved grandchildren grow up. Yet, the truth is that he's right here. The boys have often felt his presence and I see white feathers frequently. Sometimes all we have is trust. I trust that we are together and I truly hope that we meet again in another life too."

As they realised the time, it was by now well after midnight, Sheila handed Elizabeth a present.

"I hope you don't mind Elizabeth, but I just had to get you this. I hope you can accept it as a house warming gift and also as a heart opening present too. It's sent to you with the greatest of love and affection."

"Thank you Sheila."

Elizabeth looked over at Sheila and as she looked into her eyes, she knew that she had permission to open it now. Opening the gift, she found a beautiful piece of literacy in wonderful calligraphy. It was surrounded by a beautiful gold painted wooden frame. It read:

'A strong woman works out every day to keep her body in shape...but a woman of strength builds relationships to keep her soul in shape.

A strong woman isn't afraid of anything...but a woman of strength shows courage in the midst of fear.

A strong woman won't let anyone get the better of her...but the woman of strength gives the best of herself to everyone.

A strong woman makes mistakes & avoids the same in the future....A woman of strength realizes life's mistakes can also be unexpected blessings, and capitalises on them.

A strong woman wears a look of confidence on her face....but a woman of strength wears grace.

A strong woman has faith that she is strong enough for the journey.....but the woman of strength has faith that it is in the journey that she will become strong.'

The tears fell as Elizabeth read the very endearing words. The whole of the poem was written on a background of the *golden lotus*. Her heart was indeed opening and blossoming too. She really appreciated the gift and knew the exact spot where she would keep it in the orangery. By following these principles, as mentioned in the poem, she knew she would continue to live a much more fulfilling life.

"I'm so grateful, thank you."

"There is no need for words dear Elizabeth, watching you flower is more than an honour. Alexander's dear wife loved reading and she once gave me a book called 'The Voice Of Silence' by Oonagh Shanley-Toffolo. I hoped you would love it. I found the quote in there."

"Sweet dreams" they both uttered to one another as they hugged before making their way to bed.

Chapter Thirty Two

Following that conversation with Sheila, Elizabeth realised that she had never had such an open conversation with her own mother. Was it simply a question of making time for her? Was it simply that her own mother's heart centre was closed? She realised that the only way to understand her mother was to *make time for her*; despite the fact that her mother rarely had a spare minute with all the events she would constantly be organising. She knew that making time for her mother was now a priority, regardless of any excuse her mother might come up with.

Elizabeth knew that she needed to see her parents and tell them about the house too. She had changed so much recently and wondered whether or not they would notice. Now seemed as good a time as any. She decided to call in to see them rather than delay, it certainly felt the right thing to do. The twins were fine with Sheila and she had stated that she wouldn't be too long anyway.

Walking through the front door, which was usually open anyway, she noticed a glass vase smashed across the floor in the hallway. She could hear an argument going on upstairs, between her mother and father.

"How could you bring HER here?" Elizabeth's mother screamed at her husband.

"She's so well-known in the village by EVERYONE. I've known for years about your affairs, I just choose not to say anything. Bringing HER here changes ALL that now."

"I didn't mean for it to happen, she just said she wanted to chat" he pleaded.

"What do you mean, you have known about all the other affairs?"

She could hear the tone in his voice change suddenly.

"You've been having affairs since Elizabeth was about three years old. When we decided not to have any more children." Elizabeth's mother was enraged.

Jason fell to his knees, as she finally let the truth be heard.

"A woman's intuition is never to be disregarded. How often have you come home from work with lipstick on your collars and so many different perfumes wafting at me? Do you think I don't notice the lipstick when I'm putting your shirts in the washing machine? There's no way, even an undercover officer, can possibly work all those hours, all those late nights. You were often so detached and our love making became lesser and lesser. I guessed a long time ago, although you always told me that your other phone was for work. I found the *third phone* in your suit pocket, when I took it to the dry cleaners. I employed a private detective to watch over your affairs. He confirmed my feelings last week. He told me about *HER* and I knew I had to come home. You can't have sex with a barrister from my firm and expect me not to know. This time is the last. I've ignored all the others, though this time I *will* file the divorce as early as possible. *Please leave NOW."* She was shouting so loudly.

Elizabeth had been quite used to them rowing, although often they would just give each other the silent treatment for a few days. Since her maternal Grandmother had passed away several months ago, the silences had worsened. However, when Grandpa was admitted to the local hospital last month with a severe lung infection, Elizabeth had known her mother was really feeling the weight of the emotional pain. She was still standing downstairs in the hallway and wondered whether to make her presence known, or simply just leave.

"You never loved me anyway" her father, Jason continued.

Guilt was definitely his next tactic as she obviously now knew about his many affairs. The irony of being watched by a private detective indeed! Why had he missed the signs?

Pauline had literally walked in on their love-making only a few minutes earlier, just as he was about to climax. He was gutted, as he had dreamed of this moment for so long. Belinda was hot and so sexy. So many of his colleagues had wanted a taste of that particular pie. He had to pull out all the stops to get his desired outcome. He had used every bit of charm and patience he could muster. Not to mention the flowers, hand-made chocolates and even a bottle of perfume, for over two hundred quid. He was sexually bereft, angry, furious, ashamed and astounded, that she had actually found out.

Enticing Belinda had been his main mission for so many long months. They had a 'hot moment' as he had described it to his mates, outside the courtroom whilst she handled a murder case. She was the barrister and he the prosecuting officer. He and his fellow officers even had quite a bet going down at the station that he couldn't pull it off. Now what would he tell them? How would he explain this situation?

"What do you mean I never loved you, of course I did, I married you didn't I?"

Pauline was so angry and could see him becoming distracted in his thoughts. She was *angry with everything,* predominantly herself for leaving herself wide open. She had known about all the other affairs, or probably the bulk of them at least. She had stayed because she assured herself that they had always put on such a great show whilst they were out in company. Being so well known in the village, she was desperate to keep up appearances. His next words threw her completely.

"I've known Elizabeth wasn't mine from the beginning. She has such dark features, dark eyes and that beautiful olive complexion. You told me you were pregnant after a few weeks of us getting together and your belly was soon swelling after that. I'm a fucking detective. There's no way she was premature when she arrived. No wonder you never allowed me to attend the ante-natal appointments with you. I've had to trace absent fathers for years. I even did a DNA test with hair samples. I've loved that child and brought her up as my own all these years. I've always loved you and yet I've always felt second best. Was he your first love? Maybe you loved her father, more than you'll ever love me?"

He was crying hysterically now. It was all Elizabeth could do to remain silent, whilst she listened to her mother's reply. The anger between them was reaching a very high pitch indeed. Elizabeth found herself in tears, though knew she had to stifle the sobs. Her mother continued her rant:

"What would you have done? I was pregnant yes, to a man who was from a very wealthy family and I knew he would never have married me. His family would never have approved of a lowly girl from a council house, marrying their son. When I found out of his wealthy background, I deliberately told him I didn't want to see him ever again. *Pushing him away from me, knowing I could never be with him was the hardest thing I have ever had to do.* Two weeks later, I found out I was pregnant. I was so confused, though I knew I had to keep my precious baby. So yes, I told him that I was in love with someone else. When he found out that I had married you, he believed me. *All these wasted years. You with your affairs and yet me with my dark secret. Our whole marriage was based on a lie right from the start. To think I supported you through your breakdown too! What a fucking waste!"*

"So you have never loved me then? *I was always second best?"*

As the moment of the truth dawned on Jason, Elizabeth could feel his heartbreak. Pauline had confirmed his worst nightmare. He really had been second best all along, although it certainly didn't excuse his meaningless affairs. They had started out as a game and now he knew just how out of control the whole thing had become.

"What a waste. What a bloody mess. I would have married you anyway. Don't you see, the affairs were just a cry for help, to get you to *notice me.* Sometimes in your sleep you'd cry out his name. *What about Elizabeth? She's still my little girl. I was there when you gave birth for Christ's sake. Please don't tell her. PLEASE. I'll leave right now and I promise never to come back, though please don't tell her."* Her father screamed to her mother.

Elizabeth could hear his sobs over the sounds of the wardrobe doors banging and the drawers opening and then being slammed shut. The familiar sound of the suitcase zipper, signalled that he would soon be leaving the house. She knew he would be coming down the stairs at any moment and would pass her in the hallway. Her Range Rover was parked on the road outside, as she had wondered when she arrived why so many cars were on the driveway. Whether or not he would see it, she wasn't sure. For now she thought it best to move into the lounge and hide behind the sofa. Whatever she was expecting today, this certainly hadn't been on the agenda!

The suitcase was snapped shut, so she moved into the lounge as quickly and quietly as she possibly could. She could hear them both sobbing. She was stunned and felt like a rabbit in the middle of the road, with the headlights of a vehicle getting ever closer. Hiding behind the sofa, as she had done in her earlier years when something had frightened her on the television, she too was by now sobbing. Holding her breath was getting harder, as she heard him slam the front door behind him.

Her mother continued to cry and was now actually wailing to herself. Elizabeth wondered whether to move upstairs or to make her a drink, even just a simple glass of filtered, cool water from the fridge. She moved from behind the sofa and looked around at the lounge. It was perfect, as always, never any dust and never anything out of place. The whole house was like a show-house. 'What a façade indeed' she thought. She sighed a long and deep, deep sigh as she reached for the tissues underneath the coffee table.

Her mother was so surprised to see Elizabeth and was most grateful for the water, as they sat on the bed together. Her make-up was streaked all over her face, her hair was an unruly mess and her whole body was shaking violently. The sobs still came, making her whole body shake and contort. Elizabeth wasn't even sure that her mother could safely hold onto the glass.

As mother and daughter sat together, Elizabeth just held her as she continued to shake. There were no words, neither was there any need for words, as the two women just held one another. Pauline knew that Elizabeth had heard the entirety of the conversation. She knew that her life-long secret was out. She felt partly relieved, though she was still in shock too, that the whole marriage had finally crumpled.

Despite the affairs and his nervous breakdown, they had always kept on, carrying on. This was certainly the straw that had broken the camel's back. She was feeling the weight of each and every hurt, with the pain of each and every affair that he had had over the many wasted years. Her feelings of inadequacy and that she was being punished for her own lies and misdemeanours, over these many long years, poured out with her seemingly never ending tears. Every breath she took was short and the more she sobbed, the deeper they seemed to be.

The two of them must have sat for at least an hour. Elizabeth needed to excuse herself to the bathroom. When she returned her mother had gone downstairs. She looked around the house and found her in the garden outside. It was a large detached house, so the garden was very private.

"I'm sorry that you had to hear all that. It's not a nice way to find out that your parent's marriage is over. I am assuming that you heard the whole conversation?" Pauline enquired.

Elizabeth simply nodded, still in disbelief that the man she had assumed was her father, *simply wasn't her biological father at all.* It was quite a lot to take in and she wondered whether or not she did actually want to know the truth relating to her origins. She would always feel that Jason was her father. Jason had always been there, well, apart from his work. She too had always suspected the affairs. They had once gone out for a meal, just her and her father, whilst her mother was working late and a woman had openly flirted with him. Rather than ignoring her forwardness, he simply seemed to be getting a buzz from her attention.

Looking back, she remembered that he had rather encouraged her too. To a young teenager at the time, she had felt very awkward and from then on, had simply just watched him more closely when he was around other women.

Interrupting Elizabeth's thoughts, Pauline continued:

"This whole marriage has just been a façade. I knew I was pregnant with you and I knew that I could never let you go. Not just because I loved your actual father, because I could 'feel' you growing inside me. I felt special and loved. I was, after all, carrying a child of love. Look at you, you're so beautiful."

She paused, taking Elizabeth's face into her hands. Elizabeth could feel her mother's shaking hands through her cheeks.

"I loved him so much you know. When I found out he was from a very wealthy background, I got cold feet. I couldn't face the possible hurt of him leaving me. So, I ended the whole thing, telling him that I never wanted to see him again. It was one of the hardest things I have ever done. Lying to the man that I had truly loved. Telling him that I had met someone else and was in love with another man. He didn't believe me of course. He even asked if I was pregnant and if I was trying to push him away. He even said that he would marry me too. I hadn't told him of my background. We always met up in his university accommodation. He would often ask about my family, though I just changed the subject. Eventually he gave up asking." Pauline was sobbing now.

"We had known each other for a little over six months. We met whilst we were at a music concert. I loved him the very first time I set eyes on him. He was so tanned, dark and handsome. His eyes met mine and he just stared at me for the next few minutes. We were both under a spell, or so it seemed. We used to see each other as often as we could. When I found out I was pregnant, I simply assumed his family would have put so much pressure on him to leave me. They might have stopped him from doing his studying. He was so gifted and obviously loved his work. I loved him too much for that. He had plans in his career and I just felt that I would slow him down. You look so much like him and you remind me of him each and every day I see you. Will you please forgive me?"

Elizabeth nodded and began to cry too. Both of them just held the other and remained silent for several more minutes.

"I'm hungry" Elizabeth suddenly said and both women started laughing hysterically.

"I could eat a scabby donkey" her mother replied.

They moved into the house and both looked through the kitchen cupboards and the fridge. There was a huge selection of foods and cheeses, salad vegetables and some fresh sea bass fillets. Without speaking, both began to prepare a salad, some freshly squeezed orange juice and Elizabeth buttered some lovely, freshly baked bread.

"Would you like to eat on the patio, or at the dining room table Elizabeth?" her mother asked.

“Outside please mum” she replied and began to set the place mats, cutlery, glasses and side plates too. Her mother put some music on the iPod. She had always loved classical guitar.

“Dominic Miller okay?”

Elizabeth had grown up with all sorts of music, though she had to agree, that he was definitely a wonderful guitarist. It was surreal. Here they were with one another, whilst her mother’s deepest secrets were out in the open. Her father had left, the marriage broken down and yet they were about to enjoy a beautiful meal.

“That fish smells absolutely delicious. What shall I use mum, just lemon juice and some butter?”

“Yes that’ll be all it needs, I only bought it fresh from the supermarket yesterday. Jason’s favourite, I thought it would be nice to have with a salad and especially being in the summer. Sometimes he likes to cook it on the barbecue”. Her mother’s voice began to fade, as she remembered that the marriage was now well and truly over. As if trying to redeem herself, she added:

“I did love him you know, Jason I mean. I just could never love him, even half as much, as I loved your father.”

Whilst they were sitting eating the meal, Elizabeth wondered how her mother would cope now that the marital façade was well and truly over. Who was this mystery man? Could he still be in the area? Would her mother find him again? Had he felt that same way that she did about him? Was he married? Did he ever find love again? Did he complete his studies? Elizabeth had so many unanswered questions and she knew that now was definitely not the time to ask her mother.

By now she was well aware of listening to her intuition. Sheila and Ted had been great teachers and she was learning, more and more by the day, to trust that all would unfold in its own sweet time. If indeed it was actually meant to be at all. For now, she wondered if her mother would be okay on her own.

"How will you manage without him mum? Sometimes it's the little things like putting the lights out, making sure the bins are emptied, the general upkeep of the house and mowing the lawn, not to mention making sure that the doors are locked at night. I know you've always felt vulnerable whenever he has worked nights."

Laughter is certainly a funny thing in times of crisis, with those words they both burst out laughing at the thought of him 'working nights.'

"Do you want me to stay the night mum? The boys are ok with Ted and Sheila."

Pauline hadn't heard her daughter refer to Sheila as anything other than the 'witch bitch,' for many years and looked over her glasses at her only child. Elizabeth replied quickly, knowing that now really wasn't the time to discuss the reasons for her impromptu visit.

"I'm okay honey, honestly I am. I have just finished a huge libel case at the courts, so to be honest I'm quite exhausted. I think I'll hop in the bath later and then hit the sack. I've booked the next few days off work anyways. I knew once this case was over, I needed to rest. Little did I know that all this would unfold today!

When the private detective phoned me to say he had seen them together and they were headed in this direction, I thought I would just call home to see what was what. I certainly never thought that he would have the balls to bring her here. Obviously I was so wrong."

There seemed little, if any, emotion in her voice. Was she just tired, weary, relieved, upset, overwhelmed, or indeed, was it something else? Elizabeth was concerned for her mother. Pauline continued:

"I think I might even visit my sister in Devon. Well, he's taken some essentials, though perhaps it's best if I'm out of the way for the next few days and then he can collect the rest of his belongings whilst I'm gone."

"Mum that sounds like a fabulous idea."

Elizabeth responded. For a woman whose marriage had just broken up after over thirty years and who had been sobbing less than two hours ago, Elizabeth was surprised at her ability to assess the situation. She was certainly aware that her mother had always been the one in control of most situations, although this seemed particularly strange, her mother was a lawyer after all.

"How do you feel Mum? What a day!" Elizabeth said without knowing just how her mother felt. Just how was she feeling? As if reading her thoughts, Pauline replied in a simple, flat tone of voice:

"To be honest, I've known for so many years and I realised in the last few weeks, just how exhausting it's been, pretending that I didn't know about the affairs. When I took the bold decision to hire the private detective I knew what the outcome would be. Now when I sit back and look at the situation, whilst talking it through with you, I think that I have been very close to my personal cracking point. I knew my life needed a reality check. Something in me just snapped. Although it was only just over a fortnight ago, I knew I had to do it to be sure. It almost felt like my sanity rested upon knowing for sure that I hadn't just imagined it all."

The exhaustion in her mother's body language now showed and she was obviously shattered. She sighed a very deep sigh before she continued:

"I have wondered so many times if he would just not come home one day. He could have eloped with any number of women. His job has been very dangerous at times too. Some of the injuries he has sustained and the beatings over the years. I've lost count of the phone calls saying 'not to worry but...blah, blah, blah.' If I know anything, I know our divorce will be for the best, probably for us both. At least I truly hope so."

Chapter Thirty Three

Elizabeth knew that her father would be devastated, at the news of their marital breakdown. Elizabeth had confided in Sheila and asked her what she thought she should do. He could have seen her Range Rover after all, on that particular afternoon parked on the roadside. She certainly wondered whether or not he knew that she had overheard their argument.

Sheila had said that she was happy to send healing to the whole situation. Her intuition was to wait and let the dust settle. She advised it was probably better for him to contact her. Be patient. Another lesson in patience then. Elizabeth was learning and that lesson could at times, be quite a challenge!

A few days later, Jason texted her to ask how she was and ask if she was she free for a chat. The text read:

'Good morning Hummingbird. Are you free for a chat? I've had some upset at work and I could really do with a listening ear. Maybe a cuddle too for your old dad? Please can we meet at our favourite bar, The Strawberry Duck? I'll be there late morning today in the beer garden outside at 11.30am. It'll be my treat and we'll sit at our favourite table under the lilac tree. Maybe then we can take a walk in the park? Much love Popsy.'

Elizabeth was quite at ease with the thought of seeing him. She remembered when he had suffered his nervous breakdown several years ago. She recalled just how old and drawn he had looked. She was a teenager then and hadn't really properly understood what had happened. Seeing her dad like that was terribly upsetting. It had lasted several months and she was so relieved when he finally began his journey returning to full health. At least now as an adult, she was better equipped to deal with seeing him upset. Or was she?

Arriving early, she ordered a glass of orange juice and just waited, admiring the flower beds and the hanging baskets. She had always loved the homely feel of this pub and felt the love from the place whilst she had been growing up. They had celebrated many birthdays and her father's promotions here too. Her thoughts drifted to those times and she wondered just what memories she wanted to hold onto. Those she should treasure and those which were ready for the recycling bin of her mind. Besides the fun of course, there had been many times when he had flirted with the ladies, when either, or both of her parents, had got drunk and upon returning home, once that door was closed, the rows would start. She took a deep breath.

"Penny for them," her father tapped her shoulder and slapped a soft kiss upon her cheek. As she turned to face him, she was relieved that he didn't look quite as rough as he had done all those years ago.

"Thank you for coming Hummer, I got stuck in traffic at the road works. My apologies for being a little late. Are the boys okay? How are you?" her father enquired.

"They're really wonderful Popsy. I'm great too. How are you?"

"Thanks for coming. I need to talk to you about a few things. I saw your Range Rover outside the house, by the road a few days ago and I was sad that I had missed you."

She knew that he was fishing now for information. He was a detective, and a very good one at that, she thought. She knew lying was not an option, neither was providing only half an answer. As their eyes met, she could already see his tears.

"You heard the whole thing, didn't you?"

"Yes dad I did."

"Oh dear God, NO Elizabeth, I'm so sorry."

"Dad, what's done, is done. Yes, I heard the whole thing. I think I must have arrived just after the barrister left. I was shocked and I hid behind the sofa, when I heard you pack your suitcase. I've been thinking of you every day, although it felt right to let you come to me, rather than for me to prompt your response."

"I'm so sorry darling that you had to bear witness to all that." The sadness was evident in his voice and his eyes were beginning to tear up too.

The love that he had for her shone through. She was grateful that the conversation was honest and raw.

"How was your mother after I left?" he asked.

"She sobbed for quite some time to be honest and seemed to calm once we had eaten. We had an open and honest chat. She admitted that it had been coming for a while. She explained that she was tired of all the pretending and the games."

"I take it that you heard the whole conversation?"

"Yes dad, I did indeed."

Elizabeth's voice faltered as she recalled his mentioning that he wasn't her natural father. Just where was this conversation going to go?

"Shall we eat first?" he asked, without any trace of emotion.

"Yes please" was her immediate answer.

The shift in the conversation was such a relief to them both. They had privacy to chat here, although he kept to small talk and asked if they could maybe take a walk in the park later to have a 'proper chat.' They ordered lunch, knowing that as usual the service would be prompt and the food delicious.

They both agreed that would be a great idea and they ate lunch in an easy manner, as they had done over these many years.

"How are Will and Ben? Are they ready for the new term in September? I'll bet they're excited for their birthday party too? How are you?" He asked in a genuine manner.

This time he really looked up into Elizabeth's eyes and he could see such a difference in her. Her eyes were more awake, they seemed brighter and so much more vibrant.

"You're glowing" he was evidently surprised, in fact his food almost fell from his mouth.

"You look radiant. Are you pregnant darling?"

"No Dad, I'm definitely not pregnant. I split with Robert a while ago and I've done lots of *thinking and reflecting*."

“I’m very sorry to hear that Elizabeth, are you okay with all that?” His concern was genuine.

“Dad I’m fine, really wonderful as you can see.”

“Well, you look fabulous Hummer and I’m delighted. How are the boys?”

“They’re really wonderful and I’ve been spending a lot *more quality time* with them. I’ve made some new friends too and I’m about to move house anytime now.”

“Really, that all sounds amazing.” His surprise was so evident.

“I’ll tell you another time dad. Today is all about you.”

They finished their meal and as per usual, it was ‘dad’s treat.’ They walked arm in arm, to the nearby park. It was a lovely sunny day and there were lots of people about. They knew a special place where it would be quieter, in the formal gardens by the greenhouse.

“Thank you for coming, it means a lot to me. Especially now you know that I’m not your real father.”

He stopped walking and looked at her. They were both obviously saddened by recent events, though she continued to reassure him.

“You’re my dad and you always will be, no matter what. You know that nothing has changed in my eyes. I’ll always love you and be grateful for all that we have shared.” He was grateful for her honesty and integrity.

“Shall we sit on the grass, by the fountain, it’s such a beautiful spot.” She was happy to let him lead the conversation and content just to listen.

“I really do still love your mother you know, despite the affairs. I hope that you’re okay with my honesty.” She nodded, as he took this signal to continue.

“I had loved her for several months, before she noticed me. She had been friends with my sister for a while and I spotted her whilst they were out dancing. She didn’t even notice me. Then I heard that she had started dating a foreigner. I knew I would have to bide my time. I was desperate for an opportunity to get to know her more. My sister said they were in love and I didn’t have a chance. I was happy to be patient.

The more they spent time together my sister Jessica saw her less and less. Then, a few months later, she phoned Jessica and asked to meet. She told her of the break up. Jess said that she was really upset and inconsolable. Jess was obviously aware of the intensity of my feelings towards your mother, so she told me straight after their conversation. I was so excited and thrilled. I’d been waiting for this day for so long and was desperate for her to notice me.” He paused briefly before continuing:

“Jess and I hatched a plan together and when eventually Pauline and I met she was very responsive. I was totally surprised, knowing that she had really deep feelings for this foreign guy. Jess said she hadn’t revealed the details of the breakup, just that Pauline had stated very clearly, that they wouldn’t be seeing each other again.”

He paused again, to check on Elizabeth's reactions and to read her facial expressions. He was a very experienced detective after all and he cared deeply for his only daughter. Sensing that she was ok for him to carry on explaining the story and was certain that Elizabeth was not upset by his honesty he continued:

"She was happy for us to walk, talk, go dancing and to be seen in public together and it wasn't long before I felt comfortable to take the relationship to the next level as it were. You're a grown woman Elizabeth, so I hope you understand." She nodded, making it clear that she understood.

"Of course, we knew there was a risk that she might get pregnant. I was a trainee officer and had a place of my own anyway. I wanted her so badly. Within weeks of us being together, her belly was swollen and she would often feel quite rough in the mornings, whenever she had stayed over at mine. If I'm truly honest, I knew that the baby wasn't mine, though I just had to be with her. I really was in love with her so much. I suggested that we get married, before she had even told me that she was pregnant and she agreed immediately. She said she only wanted a small wedding and I was happy to give her anything she so desired."

Elizabeth listened to his honesty and she could feel the emotion in his voice too. From time to time his eyes welled up with tears. He would simply take a deep breath and just carry on. She remained silent and patient, as the story continued. Previously, her parents had told her that it was a whirlwind romance and that her mother had become pregnant straight away. It was a shotgun wedding, though it was obviously meant to be.

"I really did love her then, honestly I was totally besotted. As time went on, she became more and more distant. I just couldn't get close to her. She started to push me away and shut me out. I concentrated on my work and I was delighted when you arrived in the world. Being there at the birth was such a wonderful experience. You had such dark skin, a mop of dark hair and the most beautiful eyes I had ever seen. Look at you! You're my angel." He turned to her and took her hand as he continued.

"I knew once you were born that my worst fears had been confirmed. Yet, at the same time, I knew I loved you with every cell in my body. I would do anything to protect you and take care of you." Elizabeth was by now crying and they were both grateful for the quiet space that the park offered them.

"Your mother was exhausted after the birth and she said she couldn't make love to me for quite some months after that. I don't know what was going on in her mind. I'm a bloke, whether it was post-natal depression, or just the fact that she was reminded of him, each and every time she looked at you, I will never know. I knew I still wanted to be with her and I definitely wanted to be with you my Hummingbird."

By now they were both in tears. They just honoured their feelings and Elizabeth remained silent throughout. From time to time, she took his hand, or rubbed his shoulder as a sign of reassurance.

"Life continued as you know. Your mother was adamant that she would attend law school and despite my best efforts to convince her otherwise, she graduated with flying colours, when you were a toddler. I hadn't wanted you to be spending all that time with her parents, though it seemed the only way. She refused to put you in nursery. We could quite easily have survived off my wage, yet she was like a woman possessed. She just pushed me further and further away. I concentrated on you whenever I was at home, though she did everything she could, seemingly to stop me from getting close to you. I knew why and looking back, maybe I should have challenged her behaviour. Maybe, thinking back, she was perhaps jealous, as I had more time with you than her? Who knows? We never discussed anything. We just carried on, carrying on. I used to love bringing you here and listening to you giggle, when I pushed you on the swings." Smiling whilst thinking precious memories from many moons ago, he continued;

"In all of the chaos you were my sanity. You always had a smile and a cuddle for your dad. Obviously my work can be very stressful and demanding at times. I always managed to leave it at work though. When I was offered promotion to an undercover agent, I thought I could handle the stress. I knew it would be tough and I knew the hours would be longer too, at times. You were at pre-school, so I thought it was better for you, rather than for you to be with your grandparents. They were relieved, they were well into their seventies by then after all." His voice had deepened again and he seemed sad as he explained:

"By now your mother and I were existing, certainly not living. We merely acknowledged one another and spoke about practical things like work, childcare, etc. She passed one exam after another, after another and was so successful in her work. Our marriage became an existence, there was little conversation, very little laughter and no joy between us. If I'm totally honest, if it hadn't been for you, I would have left years ago. I have to explain something to you

Elizabeth. Before I do, *please can I ask for your forgiveness?" He was pleading with her now.*

Elizabeth had absolutely no idea in which direction the conversation was now heading, as she noted such a distinctive change in his tonality. His whole demeanour had changed so suddenly, his eyes were so, so sad. She nodded, rather than try to speak, as she could feel a huge lump appear in her throat, so that her voice seemed to have disappeared. For the first time in what seemed a long time, she sensed fear.

"I met someone before I met your mother Elizabeth. She was a fiery creature and very passionate. We had dated about eighteen months, before I met your mother and it was lust, rather than love. Inevitably, she got pregnant and she told me she was having an abortion. I had no say in the matter at all and I was greatly saddened. I knew I didn't want to be with her and would have agreed to the abortion, rather than get married to a woman who was loose, let's say. She dumped me there and then that night. She sent me a letter a week later, to say that the baby had been naturally miscarried anyway. She stated very clearly that she wanted absolutely nothing more to do with me and that I was never to contact her again. I vowed to myself after that, that I would never be with anyone, unless it was for love, nothing less. What a tangled web we weave."

He let out the biggest and deepest sigh that she had ever heard.

"Let's walk a while Hummingbird" he requested.

As he arose and reached to grab her hand, she took it. She was glad to see that old, familiar smile on her father's face. His eyes were still watery and she knew that by listening to him, he had released so many of his past emotions. Now, having experienced her own reflections and allowing her own self-forgiveness, she understood herself more and thus she understood that this was his personal journey towards self-forgiveness. She didn't feel sorry for him, rather she felt deeply saddened, that life had seemed to throw him a huge curved ball or two.

"Do you mind if I tell you about John?" He asked.

"Of course not, please do dad." John had been her father's best friend in the police force and they had a few close calls over the years. John was always known as 'Uncle John' to her. She got along great with his wife too. She was an Irish lady, elegant and tall, always stylish and had funny, crooked teeth. To a little girl, they seemed scary at first, although over time they seemed less and less so. Elizabeth smiled as she remembered his wife owned the local café and her being so cheery all the time. Sometimes after school, he would collect her and take her for her favourite hot chocolate and a 'slice of the very best chocolate cake in the whole world.' Jason looked over to his daughter and knew what she was thinking. They both smiled at those precious memories.

"It broke my heart to watch my dearest friend John lose her to cancer you know. We would have long conversations whilst we were out on surveillance. For two coppers who were supposed to be big men, we were such softies when she passed away. That was the beginning of the end for him you know. She could never have children and they would have loved to be parents. Of course it made me even more grateful that I had you in my life." He smiled at her, as they continued to walk towards the maze.

"She had a heart of gold that woman and in a way, I envied the love they shared. Funny old world, I had the perfect daughter and he had the perfect wife. That's why I took you around there as often as I could. So I could share you with them both. You know how much they loved you."

She nodded whilst wearing her 'huge little girl' grin. Those memories had indeed been very precious. The love between them was so tangible and honourable. Having the café meant that Tara was known to so many and loved by so many too. Everyone was made welcome in there and any surplus food was always given to the homeless, at the end of the day.

She would even open a soup kitchen at Christmas. John loved her dearly and when she passed away, the funeral was absolutely spectacular. There were even fireworks. The main street where the café was sited had been sectioned off, as a sign of profound respect. The flowers along the pavement were testimony to a woman 'with a heart as big as a planet,' as John would often remind them.

"As you know, within just a matter of weeks, John had collapsed at work, whilst he was working with me. Luckily, we had just attended a massive road traffic accident and the paramedics were still on the scene. I held his hand, whilst I watched my best friend die right there in front of my very eyes. I felt totally helpless and as you know, I had the breakdown soon after." She listened patiently, as she reached for the bottle of water in her handbag. She passed it across to her father.

"Someone once said, 'it's either a breakdown, or a breakthrough.' Losing Tara was so hard to endure, though losing two of the most precious folk in my life, was just too much to bear. During my breakdown, I found spending time in the hospital was peaceful and although I only saw you on odd occasions, I had time to reflect upon my life. By this point, I had had too many affairs to mention and I was so full of guilt. Through the counselling and psychotherapy sessions, I began to see life through a different perspective." He paused for a moment:

"One day, Chris, my therapist, hypnotized me and so much was revealed. I was regressed back to my early childhood, I was once again a small boy. I was scared and I was in a dark space. Chris had to really coax it from me, as to where I was. I remember shaking violently in the chair through that session. I wept uncontrollably too.

As it unfolded, I realised that I was hiding under the stairs of our first childhood home. We had moved within months of this particular evening's happenings. I recalled hearing my younger brother being beaten by my step-father. You probably remember me telling you that my real father had been killed in a freak accident, many years earlier. The screams I heard, whilst my brother yelped out in pain, were deeply upsetting to me. My whole body was contorted throughout the session."

His emotion was clearly evident in his voice, the sadness and guilt too, she intuited. Eventually, once Elizabeth had squeezed his hand as a sign of reassurance, he found the strength to continue:

"As a youngster, listening to the beating and hiding in the cupboard space, I curled my body over more and more, whilst cuddling a teddy bear in my arms. In my state of shock and horror, I pretended the teddy was my four year old brother. Hiding in the dark cupboard, I became aware that this and the other beatings, would probably lead James on to having a most destructive life. Maybe as a gambler, or an alcoholic. I also knew that I would be completely unable to assist my beloved brother. The sounds of the beating continued. It was horrible and I felt so useless.

I was always so intuitive and had experienced what I can only describe as 'a bad feeling' throughout that particular day. I often felt my brother's emotional pain. We were far too young to understand the effects of alcohol, nor the need for it." As Jason continued and the story unfolded she listened patiently.

"We had arrived home from school and as usual we were play fighting in the lounge. James had pretended to fall down and had landed on the side table, smashing both the table and the expensive bottle of whisky too. Dad was furious that the noise we made, had awakened him from his much needed sleep after the previous night-shift. When he saw the broken glass and the bottle, not to mention the treasured antique side table, he just went into an immediate rage. I tried, just as I had done many times before, to get him off James, though it was completely fruitless. Hearing James' screams, I just ran and hid under the stairs, in the cupboard. Our mum was nowhere to be seen. I guessed that she was probably at work, as she was a nurse working various shift patterns too." He was shaking now and tears ran freely down his cheeks.

"I remembered hearing a huge thump and a few minutes later the front door was opened. I cried in hysterical shame, at not having been able to assist my younger brother. To be honest, I had tried so many times previously to distract dad, or to take a beating for my brother and failed miserably. Dad was always like a man possessed, he wanted James to suffer, never me.

Ten days later, my brother's body was found along the river bank. I had completely blocked it all out. As Chris patiently coaxed the details from me, my shaking began to slow and my breathing eased too. The body was too badly decomposed when they had found it, thus the evidence was lost. This meant my brother never got the justice that he so deserved." He was so obviously full of grief, as he continued the sad story through deep breaths:

"As the memories returned, I remembered that my step-father never touched a drop of whisky, nor any other alcohol, after that evening's events. He refused to even allow my mother to drink. Alcohol was never allowed in the house ever again. She removed all James's photos and as the memories came back to me, I had even blocked out the funeral. Although it had only been a simple affair, I was stunned at those recollections. I had long forgotten too, that they had ordered a police search for several days earlier. The mind is a very powerful thing indeed. My poor brother." His grief was obvious as he shared his painful memories:

"Obviously, as a youngster I was never allowed to see the body. As the revelations continued, I remembered being under the stairs and making a vow that I would train hard to be physically very fit, becoming a great sportsman, as you know. I also vowed that I would become a police officer, to protect and serve the community, especially children. That's another reason why I could never leave you, even though I knew in truth that I was your step-father, or surrogate father. So many times, I have wanted and wished I had been your real father, my dear little Hummer." She was relieved that his tone had become a little lighter now.

"I somehow also then had an inner knowing that my brother would never be able to *trust anyone in a relationship enough to be able to love fully and live happily. It pained me so much that if he had lived, he would never feel that he deserved to be loved and couldn't receive love either.* The extent of the destructiveness would also mean that he was unable to welcome beautiful things into his life such as health, vitality and success. Through the deep revealing hypnotherapy session, I recognised that I felt that *if my brother couldn't receive abundance into his life, then neither could I.*

For the very first time Elizabeth, I can now see how this has led me to sabotage my life and most of my relationships, all completely without my conscious knowing.

James had always been mum's favourite as the youngest son. I was always used to being second best. I truly cannot believe what I have put up with in my life. My affairs were a cry for help. Peace of mind, all I am looking for is peace." He sighed once again as he reached to hug Elizabeth. They both held each other closely as she began to understand how hard his life had been right from the beginning it seemed. She was grateful for his honesty and that he had stayed in a seemingly fruitless marriage for so many years. She loved him dearly. He continued:

"Within hours of that hypnotherapy session the healing process began. To be honest it was such a huge relief. I had lost two of my very best friends and was still in a most unhealthy marriage. The affairs stopped for a while, then started up again and once I met the barrister, I just couldn't resist and allowed my wiser self to be ignored. You know the rest."

He took his head into his hands and just breathed deeply whilst he sobbed and sobbed.

Now that her father had explained his life story through his sobs and tears, the truth was dawning on Elizabeth. The reason her mother had always favoured the vicar and had always lived by obligation was because she felt obliged to work closely with him and within the church community, perhaps she had felt that she might go to hell otherwise for her 'cardinal sin.'

Her mother was afraid that Jason would find out her secret and of course he had actually known all these years. His shock at her initial betrayal and his own feelings in relation to his lost brother had led him from one affair to another and yet they had never spoken about it. They just became more and more distant and both just tolerated this behaviour.

So many lies Elizabeth thought about her life – even from the very beginning.

Chapter Thirty Four

Elizabeth's father had always called her his Hummingbird. Maybe it was time to do some research she thought. As she began to read the significance of this most beautiful creature, she finally began to understand.

'THE HUMMINGBIRD

As a power animal the hummingbird means;

You need to be very flexible with the twists and turns your life will take in the next few days.

Put more sweetness in your life – you need it.

You're going through some very heart-opening kinds of experience, and you'll quite naturally draw more and more love into your life.

Openly express the love you have and feel for those important people in your life.

Give yourself the gift of as many flowers as you can, spread them around your home, and enjoy their sight and fragrance throughout the days to come.'

'THE HUMMINGBIRD

JOY

Hummingbird, Joyful little sister, Nectar you crave

All the sweetness, of the flowers, Is the love you gave.

Hummer brings a vibration of pure joy. ...Hummingbird feathers open the heart. Without an open and loving heart, you can never taste the nectar and pure bliss of life.

If Hummingbird is your personal medicine, you love life and its joys. Your presence brings joy to others. You join people together in relationships that bring out the best in them. *The Hummingbirds mission is to spread joy or be destroyed.'*

Those last few words really brought Elizabeth to a huge point of realisation. Her life had not been filled with joy. Each day she had sought to find blame, guilt, sadness, fear or any other negative emotion, rather than *embracing the potential joy that one single day* could bring to her and her sons. Vowing right there that she would *live in the present moment,* she felt such a lightness wash over her whole being. Her knowing was indeed cemented from that day.

She recognised now that joy was the only way forward. Under no illusions that she had so much more to learn, she knew that by having patience and kindness with herself, she had the tools needed for the journey. Watch this space she thought as she remembered Ted's words of wisdom; *'Enlightenment is when both physical and higher chakras are aligned.'*

Elizabeth's journey to enlightenment was definitely well underway....

BIBLIOGRAPHY

"The Voice Of Silence" Oonagh Shanley Toffolo

"Medicine Cards" Jamie Sams and David Carson

"Animal Spirit Guides" Steven Farmer

"The Book Of Job" Dale Stafford

Author's Note

I truly hope that you have thoroughly enjoyed the read. It's been a real pleasure to write. I started the book in October 2016 but then went through many changes personally. In April 2017, I restarted it with great vigour. Within a few weeks it was finished.

It was my fiftieth birthday on June 4th and I even added some inspiration to the text before celebrating my birthday lunch with my dear family. It feels as though this book has been a precious gift to me. As the characters have unfolded and the story has taken various twists and unexpected turns, I've delighted as I have watched it flower and blossom.

It is the first work of fiction I have written. Initially having reached over thirty thousand words in May, I thought I ought to ask for a second opinion from my close and trusted friend Peter Sanderson. As a journalist, TV producer and director I felt that Peter was a great choice. He devoured it within two days and said he couldn't wait to read the next chapters. His honesty was so touching and without a doubt, I knew that I had to continue. Wild horses wouldn't have stopped me to be honest.

Most people do not see the dedication that goes into the writing of a book and the self-discipline, courage and determination needed to continue to its ending. This project has been a complete joy. I truly hope that you find it as addictive and enjoyable, as did my trusted companions who were asked to proof read and share their wisdom.

My blessed thanks to you all.

M L Curtis

Testimonials

"A mesmerizing and compelling read, this book is a real page turner. I was hooked from the very beginning. I'm looking forward to the next book already.
Reflections of a Hummingbird takes you on a powerful journey of self-healing, with the opportunity to help you reclaim power over your own life path to finding your true destiny."
Melaney-Ann Ward

"This is ML Curtis's fourth book and the first novel. I don't often read fiction so I didn't know what to expect. This book held me gripped all the way through and left me wanting more, which I hope will be forthcoming! I love the way ML shows the same events through the eyes of the different characters and I was fascinated by the way the practical application of spiritual practices are described.

I found myself identifying with the characters and relishing the details of everyday life which are described so well. For me, this book has everything - and more!
Esmee Grossman.

"It was an honour to be asked by my friend to read the latest book before it went to the printers. I can honestly say it is a great read. I really enjoyed this book, got into the characters and the story very quickly unlike some books that take ages before you identify with the story line. Straight away you are taken out of yourself and into their lives. Thank you, I really Thoroughly enjoyed it, it will make a lot of people stop and think, doing a double take on their own lives. Best wishes."
Margaret Miller.

Sometimes in life when everything starts getting just too much for us, our bodies just succumb to an illness or get damaged and we are forced to stop and take stock. In this, Mary's first novel, it is a sprained ankle that sets a life-changing wheel in motion. Mary very cleverly manages to present her philosophy for leading a fully enriched life through the main characters in a series of real life situations. This made it so much easier to take the messages on board than trying to understand "text books" on the subject.

As the story unfolded I was seeing the strengths and weaknesses of the characters in myself and a number of my friends. It helped me to shed some new light on some of my own issues. I also got so involved in the book that I began trying to predict what was going to happen next and feeling a bit smug when proved right .... and then ... the end.... How can Mary do this to me? When's the sequel coming out?

Reading this book could seriously change your life and it's a lot less painful than having to sprain your ankle to do so. Thank you Mary!!
Tony Johnson